PRAISE FOR SARA MESA

"With short, propulsive chapters, Sara Mesa creates an unforgettable gothic landscape, centered on the mysterious and menacing Wybrany College, that twists in ways that unsettle and thrill. In *Four by Four*, Mesa's sentences are clear as glass, but when you look through you will be terrified by what you see."

—Laura van den Berg, author of *The Third Hotel*

"The atmospheric unraveling of the mystery will keep you turning the page; the ending will leave you stunned—Mesa's *Four by Four* is a tautly written literary thriller that juxtaposes the innocence of children with the fetish of control; a social parable that warns against the silence of oppression and isolation through its disquieting, sparse prose."

—Kelsey Westenberg, Seminary Co-op

"Stylistically, *Four by Four*'s narrative structure is both dazzling and dizzying, as its perfect pacing only enhances the metastasizing dread and dis-ease. . . . Mesa exposes the thin veneer of venerability to be hiding something menacing and unforgivable—and *Four by Four* lays it bare for all the world to see."

—Jeremy Garber, Powell's Books

"Very few authors evoke a visceral reaction with prose in the way that Sara Mesa does. . . . *Four by Four* sounds an alarm on the dangers of power, privilege, and the self-delusions told in order to hide complicity. A work of high gothic art, *Four by Four* solidifies Mesa as one of the strongest female voices in contemporary Spanish literature."

—Cristina Rodriguez, Deep Vellum Books

"This is a linguistically precise, stylistically spare, and emotionally devastating look at the corrosive effect of abuse and ~~~ e, perfect for fans of Shirley Jacks~~

—*Shelf Awareness*, starred re

"Like Buñuel's *Exterminating Angel*, or even Bong Joon-ho's *Parasite*, the rich are left rotting in a swamp of their own design. . . . *Four by Four* is an uncomfortably real look into the absurd world of the bourgeoisie. It is so complex and layered that, to reach a full understanding, one may have to read it two or even three times. Not a single character, after all, is what they seem."

—Noelle Mcmanus, *The Women's Review of Books*

"A meticulously constructed and chilling study of desire and influence."

—*Kirkus Reviews*

"Mesa presents a painful exploration of inequity, cruelty, and the immeasurable cost of belonging."

—Terry Hong, *Booklist*

"The language is short and precise, as if from a dream, yet each character has a distinctive point of view, sometimes cold and distant, sometimes uncomfortably intimate. . . . *Four by Four* is a mystery among mysteries. Things are deeply wrong at Wybrany College, but it's not clear-cut how to fix them. Each character must fight both their innate human tendencies and the forces acting against them, and as in the real world, the solutions are personal."

—T. Patrick Ortez, *World Literature Today*

"Sara Mesa. Don't forget that name. The finalist for the 30th Premio Herralde de Novela. Read it. Share it. Talk about it. Open the book and begin. You won't be able to put it down."

—Uxue, *Un libro al día*

"An original novel full of talent, an oppressive fable in which nothing is what it seems and in which its author shows herself to have some striking credentials: it is about somebody capable of creating a sophisticated nightmare using only one stroke of fine line."

—Pablo Martínez Zarracina, *Bilbao*

Among
the
Hedges

Sara Mesa

TRANSLATED FROM THE SPANISH
BY MEGAN MCDOWELL

OPEN LETTER
LITERARY TRANSLATIONS FROM THE UNIVERSITY OF ROCHESTER

Originally published by Editorial Anagrama S.A. as *Cara de pan*, 2018

Copyright © Sara Mesa, 2018
c/o Indent Literary Agency
www.indentagency.com

Translation copyright © 2021 by Megan McDowell

First edition, 2021
All rights reserved

Library of Congress Cataloging-in-Publication Data: Available.
ISBN-13: 978-1-948830-39-3 │ ISBN-10: 1-948830-39-6

This project is supported in part by an award from the National Endowment for
the Arts and the New York State Council on the Arts with the support of
Governor Andrew M. Cuomo and the New York State Legislature.

Support for the translation of this work was provided by
Acción Cultural Española, AC/E

AC/E
ACCIÓN CULTURAL
ESPAÑOLA

Printed on acid-free paper in the United States of America.

Cover Design by Alban Fischer
Interior Design by Anthony Blake

Open Letter is the University of Rochester's nonprofit, literary translation press:
Dewey Hall 1-219, Box 278968, Rochester, NY 14627

www.openletterbooks.org

AMONG THE HEDGES

Part One

THE PARK

SHE IS SO CAUGHT OFF GUARD the first time that she jumps at the sight of him. The girl is sitting with her back against a tree and reading a magazine when she hears the approaching steps, the crunch of dry leaves, and then he's standing right there in front of her. He's perhaps a bit taken aback, but not shocked to find her there, hidden behind the hedges. The old man apologizes—I didn't mean to scare you! he says—and asks her what she's reading. Between one thing and the other—between the apology and the question—the girl has time to react. This, she replies, showing him the magazine, a women's magazine. Maybe, she thinks, when he sees this magazine that is obviously not for little girls, he'll think she's older than she is and she'll avoid the dreaded question—what are you doing here, at this time of day?—though in fact the old man merely smiles and peers tentatively at the magazine. At first it seems like he's going to take it—his fingers hesitate, reach for it—but the gesture withers out and the hand falls, spent, to his side. The old man looks at the girl now, then back at the magazine, the girl, the tree, the little hideout in the hedges, and finally speaks, saying: What's in the magazine? What's it about? The girl angles away from the tree trunk, leaning forward over her bare, crossed legs. The dry grass has left impressions on her skin, little red spots from all the hours of sitting on the ground. Girl stuff, she says. Stuff about music and video games, and also movies and clothes, music gossip. Gossip about singers and actors, I mean, their lives and stuff like that. I don't know much about all that, he says, but his tone holds no creeping reproach or scorn. I read magazines, too, he says. But mine are about birds! Birds? the girl murmurs, disconcerted, wondering if maybe, when he says *birds*, the old man is referring to something else, that it's actually an innuendo. This thought makes her more suspicious and she even entertains the thought of running away, but the old man is speaking again and his words sound guileless. Not just about birds, he explains, they're really about animals in general; magazines specifically about birds aren't so easy to find, and plus, they're expensive! He used to subscribe to one that doesn't exist anymore, it was delivered to his house every week, and that was where he learned everything he knows about birds, which is a lot! The old man talks like a kid—self-absorbed and excited—and the girl looks at him curiously. In the mornings, in that park—he continues—you can easily see a hoopoe and also, more and more often, a ring-necked parakeet or even a Eurasian collared dove, hasn't she noticed? The girl shakes her head. She doesn't even know what a normal dove looks like, she thinks, so how could she tell the difference between that and a Eurasian one? She also thinks: what a strange man. She looks at him sidelong but doesn't raise her head entirely—he's still standing and she's still sitting. She eyes him up and down, taking in his elegant laced shoes, his light-colored dress pants and matching jacket—heavy in spite of the heat—the sporty little backpack that hangs from one shoulder, so at odds with the rest of his outfit. She observes his chubby, freckled hands, his small, blond head, his little wire-rimmed glasses and mustache, his hair standing crazily on end. She finds him funny, but not enough to let her guard down. The old man keeps talking. There are exotic species that were never seen here before, he explains, species that adapted to their new environment and became a danger for the endemic ones—he gets stuck on the word *endemic* and has to repeat it three times before he pronounces it correctly. But he doesn't mind them, he continues, he likes all the species, the ones from here and the ones from elsewhere, he doesn't care where they come from, they're all truly extraordinary! He is thoughtful for a few seconds, and that's when his expression changes. His eyes grow round and large as if something were just dawning on him, and his jaw trembles slightly. I'm being annoying, he says, and he apologizes for the second time. No, no, says the girl out of politeness, but he insists, distressed: he always talks too much, and if no one stops him he goes on and on. Someone has to tell him, he adds disconsolately, he just doesn't realize on his own! He looks to either side, bows his head abruptly and says goodbye to the girl, who doesn't know what to say or do. When she sees him turn around and bumble away through the hedges, she's relieved to be alone again. Though he didn't seem like he'd be a problem, she thinks. He was nothing at all like the men she's met on other occasions, the dangerous ones.

The old man reappears at more or less the same time the next day. The girl no longer finds him amusing, and it occurs to her that he could be spying on her. Nevertheless, the man's attitude is as shy and respectful as it was the day before. He's wearing the same clothes, the same expression of meek astonishment. This time he asks if he can sit down for a bit. He settles in as far away from her as the hideout's size will allow: there can't be more than six feet between the row of hedges and the tree. Legs crossed, hands on his knees, he smiles at her, takes a deep breath. You're not reading today?, he asks, but he asks in a way that he could have asked anything else, thinks the girl, a question to break the silence. She opens her backpack and takes out a book, one she had to buy for school, and she hands it to the old man, who reaches over to take it. Do you like it?, he asks, flipping through the pages. Yeah. Depends. I get distracted. He smiles again. What, you get really bored? No, she says. And then she adds: just normal, I get bored the normal amount.

He's never liked reading. Only his magazines about birds, he says, or about nature in general. But with novels he gets lost. Whenever he starts to read one, his head goes somewhere else, not because he gets distracted, but quite the opposite—because he gets too deep into the story! He gets attached to the protagonist, or some other character, and he imagines they're him, or he's them. He can't help but change the story, imagine what he would do if he were in their place, choosing one path or another for himself. Sometimes he imagines himself as several characters at the same time, and then it's all a big mess. By the time he realizes, he's reading without following the story at all. He can read entire pages without understanding a thing!, while his thoughts just wander freely. Doesn't that happen to her? The girl shrugs her shoulders. She doesn't like to read either, she admits.

Then why do you have a book in your backpack?

A blackbird slips through the bushes, sees them, and flaps away as fast as it can, making a racket. The bird distracts the old man and gives the girl time to think of a valid reply to such a silly question. Why does she have a book in her backpack? She's not going to mention school. If she does mention it, he'll ask what grade she's in and then do the math. She can say that it's her brother's book. A book she borrowed from her brother's room—it's a logical answer since her brother has tons of books, and now that he's gone she can borrow as many as she wants. She's about to say just that, that the book belongs to her brother, when the man gets up, brushing bits of grass from his pants and stretching his limbs as if his whole body hurt. Oof, he complains, his body isn't meant for sitting cross-legged on the ground anymore! The girl wonders just how old this old man is. This old man who, incomprehensibly, still has not asked her age.

She's thought about changing hideouts, but she hasn't found another as good as this. Though the tree trunk is hard and rough, it has a fairly smooth depression where she can lean against it comfortably. The branches are covered with small, soft leaves of a silky green that extend to the sides and form a kind of shelter, dappled with light and shade. The girl just has to cross through where the hedges are less thick, just sparse enough to let someone pass. Once inside, between the hedge and tree, all she has to do is sit down and no one can see her, not even someone who passes very close by—as long as they don't peer over. She can pee right there if she ever needs to, off to one side, because it's nearly certain no one will see her. Besides, the park is almost empty at that time of day. She arrives around eight-thirty, walking fast, head down, trying to move with confidence—the kind of confidence she's seen in older girls, in teenagers—backpack on her back, dragging her feet, headphones on. No one ever stops her, and only occasionally does she glimpse the park and garden workers in the distance, uniformed and busy. At eleven she eats her snack, at one she gets a little drowsy— she doesn't plan it like that: it's just that the midday heat puts her to sleep—and at two she's ready to get up again and head home. She crosses paths with the kids coming out of the nearest school—and with the parents or grandparents who lead them by the hand—but no one notices her: she's a big girl next to those children, an older kid who no longer needs anyone to pick her up. It's possible there are other hideouts in the park—all those rows of hedges must conceal some—but she hasn't been able to find them, and it's not a good idea to prowl around suspiciously. During the first days, in another park that was larger but also more crowded, two different men had approached her and asked lots of questions. One of them had even grabbed her arm and tried to convince her to take a walk with him. There'd also been an elderly woman who wanted to know why she was there, whether she wasn't expected somewhere else, and whether her parents knew about her little excursion—*excursion*, here, struck her as an exaggerated and malicious word. The girl decided to look for another park, quieter and farther away, where no one would ask questions. She's been in this hideout for several days now with no interruption, save for the old man, who has shown up two days in a row. But this, she thinks, the fact that he happened to be here two days in a row, doesn't mean he'll come every day.

But, obviously, he does.

This time, before sitting down, he takes a cloth handkerchief from his pocket, unfolds it ceremoniously and lays it on the grass. So I don't get dirty! he says, but she looks closely and sees that he's already dirty. The same light-colored pants as before—so poorly suited to a walk in the park—are covered in dust, their hems blackened from dragging on the ground. The old man is sweating and a lock of hair is plastered to his forehead, the lenses of his glasses are all smeared, and he has a small pair of binoculars hanging around his neck that only accentuate his outlandish appearance. Still, in spite of his scruffiness, there's something about him that reminds her of an old neighbor of hers, a very distinguished professor, very elegant—that's what her mother had said, that he was very *distinguished* and *elegant*; it's something to do with the way he pushes back the lock of hair, and it's in spite of the freckles on his hands, the redheaded paleness of his skin, so rare.

What is he looking for in her? Is he trying to get at the burning question? Her age? The fact that a girl her age is there, in the park, sitting against a tree at this time of day? If that's what this is about, the old guy is beating around the bush before trapping her, like a predator that spots its prey but takes its time before pouncing. Maybe he's hoping to win her trust so that later on, when she least expects it, he can catch her unawares.

This is what the girl thinks, confusedly, when she's alone, but when he's there with her, when she observes him carefully, she's not so sure. Maybe he's just bored, an early retiree who doesn't quite know what to do with his time, a pain in the neck, a wimp, even a dirty old man. But not a snitch. He doesn't seem to have it in for her.

The old man puts a finger to his lips and closes his eyes. He concentrates on listening to the song of a bird flying above them. The girl stays silent, waits on pins and needles. A robin, the man finally announces, triumphant.

She's annoyed by all the liberties he takes. This was her spot, hers alone—aren't there any others in the park?

The next day he brings her a towel. A thin towel, old and rough, beige with brown designs on the ends. When he takes it from the backpack to offer it to the girl, she catches a whiff of cheap detergent. This way you won't have to sit on the ground, says the old man. There are a lot of bugs, and the grass is itchy! The girl takes the towel cautiously. The truth is that she's thought about sneaking one from her own house, but her mother, so organized and infallible, would notice it missing immediately. Plus, in her family they don't use such old, thin towels. All their towels are fluffy, very large and soft, *hundredpercentcotton*—as her mother always says—same as the *hundredpercentcotton* sheets and the *hundredpercentcotton* underwear: they're the best, but they're no help to the girl because they're too bulky to hide in her backpack. So she thanks him, but mumbles: I can't take it home with me. Why not? Why can't you take it home with you? My mother would ask where I got it, she replies. It's so obvious! The old man raises an eyebrow skeptically, as if he didn't entirely understand. So tell her the truth! Tell her I gave it to you, she won't think you stole it, will she? The girl looks at him in silence with the towel still in her hand, hanging down to the ground. The old man is standing too, looking back at her in surprise. He must have noticed a change in her, a cautious distance. What's wrong?, he finally asks. Did I do something wrong? The girl shakes her head. No, no, it's just that she doesn't like for people to worry over her. Why not? What's wrong with worrying about other people? The girl doesn't reply. She spreads out the towel and sits in the middle, not leaving any room for the old man. He, in turn, sits down on his ridiculous little handkerchief, as far away from her as possible. Does the old man expect her to invite him to sit next to her, on the towel, side by side, like two friends having a picnic? Is it rude if she doesn't? She is so rattled that she no longer knows the right thing to do: neither the right thing in general nor the right thing for her, at that moment.

The old man asks her if she doesn't read magazines anymore. Not today, she says. He asks if she likes animals, and she says yeah. If she likes music, and she says of course. He asks what kind of music, and she replies I don't know. He asks if she wants him to leave, and she says I don't care. Then he goes quiet, the silence grows and everything goes slack: even the murmur of a mower in the distance suddenly cuts off. The girl feels all the weight of uncertainty, and she looks up to scrutinize him. She examines his face for the first time, focuses on his eyes, tiny behind his glasses, and on his thin mustache that curves slightly upward—so old-fashioned, she thinks, no one has a mustache like that these days. It must be a hard look that she gives him, because he is unable to meet it. He lowers his head, uses his arms to push himself to his feet. He picks up his handkerchief and folds it neatly, puts it into his pants pocket. An old towel is an old towel, he says, it shouldn't be that complicated! He brought it to help her, not make problems for her. He sighs, aggrieved. I'm being annoying again!, he says. Why does he stick his nose in when no one asked him to? The girl doesn't know what to do now. She looks at him anxiously, asks if he wants the towel back. Yes, of course, since you don't want it, he replies. The girl hands it back and he stuffs it haphazardly into his backpack along with the rest of his things. I'm being annoying!, he repeats several times, and then, in a quieter voice: it was just a towel.

When he leaves, the girl lies on the ground—directly on the grass, now—and looks up at the sky, thoughtful. Is he angry? Will he tell on her? What should she have done to keep him from telling? Not offend him? Accept his absurd gift, that old towel that smelled of a thousand washes? Did she have to be so rude?

The blue framed by the green of the tree shifts, overtaking the silhouetted leaves. Each branch is outlined in red; she's not blinking, and the light burns her pupils. She keeps her eyes open as long as she can, then squeezes her eyelids shut and plays at chasing the little colored spots. The image of the old man is burned into her retina, too. It's not easy to get rid of. He's a very strange old man.

It's almost noon when he appears. Although part of her is already celebrating having finally gotten rid of him, another part, more hidden and incomprehensible, is pleased to see him. The old man is startled, like he didn't expect to find her there, as if she were once again a novelty, or a discovery. I didn't think you would come back!, he says. I came to find you yesterday and the day before, but you weren't here. I thought you were still mad! Mad? It takes the girl a second to understand, to piece it together. The old man didn't realize it was a weekend. She doesn't go to the park on Saturdays and Sundays, she doesn't need to hide on those days. If the old man hasn't figured that out yet, it means he isn't suspicious. This reasoning, rather than soothing her, offends her a little. So, there was no need to pretend? What an idiot. She grows bolder, speaks easily, now with no mistrust. I don't come on the weekends, she says. Oh, okay, he murmurs, and why is that? The girl stares straight into the old man's eyes, so small through his glasses. Because there's no school, she says. The old man scratches his head, still not understanding. She finds herself forced to continue, almost angrily: I come here instead of going to school. His lips part, as if he were going to say something and then—on second thought—he doesn't. He asks if he can sit down. She nods.

The old man takes his place very slowly, sitting on the towel that he's brought again, but doesn't offer her now. He crosses his legs with difficulty and reflects. We see each other here because you skip school, he says at last, and also: maybe that's not good! What's not? she asks, and thinks, but doesn't say: what is it that's not good? Skipping school, or for the two of them to see each other every morning? I don't need to go to school, she says. I don't need the stuff they teach there, that stuff in particular, I don't need it, or at least I don't need anyone to teach it to me. I can learn it by myself: all the things, everything, it's already online and in books. The old man asks her until what age a person has to go to school. She swallows. Does that change things, if the old man knows that or not? It's obligatory until sixteen, she says. Until fifteen, actually: the day you turn sixteen you can leave if you want. And you?, he asks, how old are you?

For a few seconds, the girl debates between lying and risking the truth, and she chooses the truth, or half-truth. Fourteen, she finally says: I'm fourteen. He looks at her as if he didn't believe her; she feels unmasked. Well, almost, she backpedals. I'll turn fourteen soon. Soon, soon murmurs the old man, shaking his head side to side. He'd thought she was older, but fourteen! Not even fourteen yet, in fact, but almost fourteen, soon-to-be fourteen . . . What's your name? The girl tells him her name and he shakes his head again. A pretty name, yes, really pretty! But she interrupts: I hate my name. Oh, well then, there's nothing else to say, if she doesn't like it they don't have to use it. He can call her Almost, if she's okay with that, or maybe Soon would sound better. She says: yes, she's okay with Soon. It reminds her of a neighbor she used to have, a neighbor named Asún, an older woman who gave her candy when they met on the stairs—she carried it in her apron pockets, which were always bulging. That was before they moved into the house, back when Soon was much younger than fourteen and they'd lived in an apartment building full of people to stop and talk to. Her neighbor's name was really Asunción, a horrible, old-lady name. But Soon, Soon on its own, Soon for soon-to-be-fourteen, sounds good, it's ingenious, it's like a secret name that the old man has thought up just for her. And this same old man now places his hand over his chest and promises, in turn—swearing with all the solemnity of a true gentleman—to tell the whole truth and nothing but the truth. His complete name—first, middle, and last—and his age—fifty-four years old. Fif-ty-four, he repeats, laughing, sing-song, not *almost* fifty-four, not *soon-to-be*, but fifty-four *now*. Aren't I old. Soon laughs too, hiding the fact that she would have believed any age he told her, whether forty-four or sixty-four—to her this man is an old man and old men have ages as variable as they are inconceivable. Can she call him that? Old Man? Sure, sure, he goes on laughing. Soon and Old Man, why not?

Old Man, are you going to tell on me? asks Soon, and *old man* does not sound like an insult at all, but quite the opposite: conspiratorial and gentle. He looks at her without blinking: tell on you for what?, he asks, and Soon doesn't know if it's a joke or if he's being serious. Does this old man not understand anything? In any case I look sixteen, when people ask me I've said I'm sixteen and they've always believed me—you yourself, Old Man, thought I was older than I was! (Although it's not true that anyone has asked her age, or that she believes she looks older than she is, and nor is her confidence genuine as she brags about her appearance—in reality, she has so many doubts.)

In the middle of October the weather is variable; in the early morning, when Soon arrives, it's still cool and the damp grass gives off a more fragrant scent, almost sweetish, which dissipates and dries up as the hours pass. But from twelve o'clock on, like now, it can even get hot, and the pits of Soon's knees start to sweat from sitting so many hours with her legs bent. Old Man crosses through the hedges—he's bent over, and once he's through, the greenery closes behind him—and he looks at her with shining eyes, pleased to find her there, as if her very presence each time were a formidable gift. Look, he says, I brought you something.

Clumsy with nerves, he takes some headphones from his jacket pocket, unrolls them, plugs them into a cell phone, and focuses on pushing the buttons, which he does very slowly. Listen, he says finally as he hands her the headphones, and she promptly fits them into her ears.

What comes through them is a woman's clear, deep voice, an ambiguous voice, slightly masculine, thunderous, but it's the clean, booming thunder of a wave crashing against a jetty, a voice that enfolds her and carries her up and then down, and in the background there's a sax, or a trumpet—Soon doesn't know—a wind instrument that blends into the voice, intertwining, instrument with voice and voice with instrument, rising and falling as if competing or dancing. She closes her eyes, listens, listens very intently, though she never entirely forgets that Old Man is watching her. When the song rises and rises and rises and finally breaks before falling suddenly to its end, she hands the headphones back and says: it's pretty. Old Man nods, smiles, thanks her. He thanks her, not the other way around, thinks Soon: it's all so strange.

Nina Simone, murmurs the Old Man, that's Nina Simone, but it's a name Soon has never heard before. It's possible that what he likes most in the world, says Old Man, after birds, or just as much as birds, is that woman's voice—and when you think about it, they're practically the same thing. She was a singular woman, he explains, spent her whole life fighting for her people, but she wasn't always well understood, and when Soon asks who *her people* were, Old Man says: black people! Soon did like the song, she wouldn't be at all opposed to listening to it again, but she's not terribly interested in the story Old Man is telling her now, full of dates and names and more dates and more names that inevitably make her attention wander. Nina Simone, says the Old Man, was a stage name, just like how the two of them assumed new names, Soon and Old Man, to escape their real ones, which are prisons. When Nina was a little girl named Eunice, the Jim Crow laws were in force—*Jiiim Crooow*, Soon slowly repeats—separate but equal, or each with his own, explains Old Man. That is, whites over here and blacks over there, no mixing, but there went little Eunice every day, off to a white neighborhood to take her piano classes, day in and day out of people cursing her and throwing stones—who did that monkey think she was, setting foot on their white sidewalks?—and even so she kept going, she was brave, and she really liked music!

Soon, whom no one curses in the street much less throws stones at, but who has decided never to set foot in school again—maybe not out of bravery, but lack of it—merely smiles and offers Old Man some chips, since she's bought a large bag and there are still some left at the bottom. Old Man sticks his hand in and scoops up the crumbs with his fingers, which he then licks very politely and delicately—not the way Soon does it when no one is looking at her, which is almost always. The scent of artificial ham flavor spreads out between them; Soon likes that he's accepted the chips and that he eats them without talking, focused on keeping the crumbs from falling onto his pants. Mmm, these are good, he says when he's finished, but they make me thirsty, don't those chips make her thirsty? Soon explains that when she gets thirsty she leaves the hideout for a moment and refills her water bottle at a drinking fountain less than ten meters away; the problem is that at that hour, more or less from one o'clock on, the water comes out really hot because the sun beats down right on the fountain. Old Man offers to buy some fresh water, or a soda, whichever she prefers, and Soon remembers her parents telling her that never, under any circumstances, should she accept gifts from strangers, although then she tells herself that water isn't exactly a gift, and that this man is no longer exactly a stranger, and also, above all, that he had accepted her chips kindly, so now she can't seem wary or ungrateful, so she says: okay, sure. But, water or soda, which do you want? Water, water. Old Man gets up, disappears through the bushes, and returns fifteen minutes later with a bottle of cold water and two more bags of chips, one for each of them.

Nina, he continues, once she was famous and earning a ton of money, was accused of tax evasion and had to leave her country—that's how the United States got rid of her! What's tax evasion?, asks Soon, and to explain it Old Man talks to her about why people pay taxes, and about the rebellion it takes to refuse to pay certain taxes. Is it acceptable not to pay the State if the State does bad things with our money, like, for example, killing people? Soon has heard her parents talking about taxes and she thinks it's mandatory to pay them, otherwise you can be thrown in jail. But what if the tax money is used to finance a war?, insists Old Man.

Nina didn't want to collaborate in the disaster of Vietnam, he says, that's why she refused to pay! Sure, reflects Soon, then it's different, although she doesn't remember what the *disaster of Vietnam* refers to—did she study it in school? . . . if so, she's forgotten!

Do you pay taxes?, she asks cautiously. Me? Old Man laughs. He doesn't work, he says, it's been years since he worked, that's why he gets confused about days, he never knows when it's Monday or when it's Tuesday, he only finds out when he goes to buy something and the stores are closed! Are you unemployed?, asks Soon. No, not exactly, he didn't say that he was out of work, but that he doesn't work, it's not the same thing. If he were jobless it would imply that he's looking to change his situation, and he's not looking for anything now, he simply doesn't work! She would like to ask him what he lives on, then, what money he used to buy the chips and the water, but, after all, how people manage to survive without a salary is none of her business, and her parents have taught her to be discreet and never ask personal questions. So she keeps quiet and listens to him talk about his Nina and everything she suffered in her life, including the violence of a bad man who never really loved her and whom he, Old Man, curses for not having been good enough for his goddess.

It's their routine now to share some junk food, a soft drink. Old Man only talks about birds or Nina Simone, he pronounces names in Latin—scientific names, he says, like

Turdus merula, Sturnus unicolor, and *Apus apus*—or in other languages—Miriam Makeba, Simone Signoret, Nelson Mandela. He lets her use his binoculars to look at the sky, and he teaches her to identify the birds that fly overhead, from the meek and dreary sparrows to the distinguished western yellow wagtail. He's brought her ornithological magazines and a hardcover beginner's guide, and he also lends her his phone so she can listen to more Nina Simone songs and look at photographs of her: Nina thoughtful, smoking, a colorful turban on her head; Nina in profile with huge silver hoop earrings; Nina with her little Lisa, both with their hair styled in complicated, braided updos; Nina at the piano and Nina singing; Nina young and Nina old; Nina with sequins in her eyebrows and eyelashes; the Nina of joyfully intense eyes, and Nina of the tortured gaze. By now he's told her Nina's entire life, from childhood to death. Though he repeats himself a lot and almost always bores her, Soon doesn't want to interrupt him because he interrupts himself, unexpectedly, when he realizes that *he's being annoying.* Soon, you have to tell me, he begs her very seriously and sadly, I don't want to be a pain, the worst thing in the world is to be a pain!, but it's true, thinks Soon, that he is a bit of a pain, even if he's also funny, not because of what he says but his way of saying it: his quick movements, his twinkling eyes, the way he runs his hand through his hair and leaves it sticking straight up, crazily. Let me clean your glasses, Old Man, she tells him, and she does it meticulously, glancing surreptitiously at his naked face, his faded blue eyes bigger and more vulnerable without the lenses, his droopy eyelids slightly swollen, purplish. He never asks about her life, doesn't pressure her to tell him anything, and he leaves as abruptly as he arrives, a little hasty and embarrassed. She is grateful for Old Man's discretion, his way of situating himself at her level and not prying, so unlike other adults. Still, she kind of wishes he would take an interest in her, show some curiosity about her life beyond the border of the hideout. Maybe because of that, without any goal in mind, she starts to make things up, to lie, and she tells him she knows how to do a ton of things that she doesn't: skate, dance, play the violin, speak French. In summers, she says, her parents rent a huge house right on the beach, huge and unkempt, and their life there is also unkempt, with crowds of visitors who show up without calling first and leave without warning. Her parents give her a lot of freedom, she can come and go and they don't ask questions, she can get up at whatever time she wants—or not get up at all—eat whatever she feels like—or not eat at all. At night she's allowed to sit with the grown-ups, and once in a while they even let her drink a glass of wine or champagne. Her father is a very celebrated doctor and her mother is a theater actress; they both have sophisticated and extravagant friends. One of those friends, a man in his thirties, tried to seduce her one morning at dawn. She firmly refused and he understood; he did the math and promised to wait five years until she came of age. For winter vacation, when they can't go to the beach house—it's an inhospitable, wind-swept coast—they pack their bags and travel the world. Turkey, Taiwan, India, Japan . . . destinations always as far-flung as they are exotic.

The fact that it's all made up is revealed gradually. She stops lying out of laziness. Reality imposes itself, and she runs out of energy to go on fabricating. Without openly admitting it, the real Soon makes her way out through that irritating false Soon. Middle-class Soon whose parents are just doing their best, their normal family vacations in summer; solitary Soon, clumsy and plagued with hang-ups; angry Soon, unfair to those around her, rude at times; misunderstood Soon; Soon with no one who listens, except now that she's at least found this man, Old Man, who only talks about birds and Nina Simone, and who never lies.

There is a constant threat from the workers who patrol the park daily in their various tasks. The ones who wear an orange uniform are working on remodeling the duck pond. They destroyed its fountain and now they're building another one, uglier but—apparently—safer. Then there are the ones in green uniforms, who are the gardeners, and who make a great racket with their lawnmowers, hedge trimmers, and weed eaters. Finally, the ones in yellow work on cleaning. They sweep leaves from the main walkways and punctually empty garbage cans. All of them—orange, green, yellow—work very responsibly and hardly ever take breaks. Soon sees them when she arrives, when their days are also just beginning, and she avoids looking them in the face when their paths cross. They're all men and they all inspire deep respect in her, not exactly because they are men, but because of what they could do if they noticed her there, alone or accompanied. When she hears them on the other side of the hedges, she holds her breath until they move off. Sometimes she catches snippets of their conversations. One complains about his wife. Another says he has a new grandson. Many of them talk about soccer. And then there are stray sentences that, taken in isolation like that, are disconcerting: "One crack with the ax and it's swept under the rug," for example. Or: "The whole cookie fad just makes me nervous, what can I say." Soon worries about them getting too close, especially when Old Man is around, when they could be overheard talking or laughing. There shouldn't be anything strange about her being there chatting with whomever she likes—a friend who could well be her uncle or father—but even so, she realizes it's best to hide.

One day when they've both stood up to say goodbye, an orange worker walks near them and looks them up and down suspiciously. Then he slowly walks away, turning back several times. Soon knows she is hanging by a thread, that sooner or later someone will come asking questions, but that sense of precariousness, rather than scaring her, grants her a certain status, a special place beside her friend, and it ties her to him, since the two of them now share a secret.

She never would have thought there were so many different birds in the city's parks. But it's just a matter of paying attention! Of training your eyes! Old Man writes them down in a notebook, in his spiky, careful handwriting from another era: 1. Blackbirds, which as she can see are everywhere; 2.

Starlings, careful, because they imitate the songs of other birds and confuse you; 3. Robins, known for their speed in assembling a nest—a gardener left his jacket hanging at nine in the morning and picked it up at one in the afternoon, with a nest in the pocket!; 4. Crested tits, useful as natural insecticides—they eat everything! 5. Serins, with their unmistakable, raucous song—there aren't many, but they make themselves heard!; 6. Willow warblers, so tiny and hard to see!; 7. Wagtails, white ones and yellow ones, always near the water, of course; 8. Goldfinches—one of them pulled the thorns from Jesus Christ's head; 9. Swifts, so hardy they sleep while they fly . . . Shall I go on? Tomorrow, Old Man, it's already a lot, she says.

He has a birdsong identification game on his phone. It's really fun, he says, let's do level one, and he presses: nuthatch, kingfisher, robin redbreast, bullfinch, magpie, wagtail, wood pigeon, great spotted woodpecker, greenfinch. Then he plays them out of order: Pi-pi-pi-prrrrr . . . Kingfisher! Good! Prii-prii-prii . . . Wagtail! Bravo! Cracruaa-cra-criaa-cra . . . Wood pigeon? No, no, listen again: Cracruaa-cra-criaa-cra . . . Great spotted woodpecker? No way! How could that be a woodpecker? The woodpecker's song is much sharper, totally different. Want to hear again? Soon's head hurts, but she tries. Greenfinch? No, no, and no. It's a magpie, listen close, it's unmistakable! But Soon is bored, she's overwhelmed, all the songs sound the same, chirps and caws, what's the difference. She feels like when she has a test at school, trying to memorize facts that don't matter to her in the slightest, with the difference that here the teacher's (Old Man's) enthusiasm seems genuine, and his patience great. So she makes an effort, repeats, and soon she graduates to level 2: lark, skylark, crested lark, bee-eater, grebe, avocet. She starts to catch the bug, to get into it, now it's not just that she doesn't want to let him down, she wants to win. When only three days later she manages to get them all on the first try, she lets herself be caught up in a silly sense of pride, smiles happily, suggests they go on to level 3, then mix up all the levels.

There's something about Old Man's way of speaking that Soon, instinctively, perceives as abnormal. For one thing, he doesn't control his volume the way he should: sometimes he speaks in whispers and she has to ask him to repeat himself—it feels like he's telling a secret, but no, he's not. Other times, his voice rises at inopportune moments and he shouts, running the risk of catching the workers' attention. Those ups and downs don't have anything to do with his mood: he doesn't speak like that because he's nervous or angry, or because he wants to give or receive orders. As the days pass, she understands that it is, quite simply, his way of expressing himself: it's a peculiar manner, grating at times, that could even come off as rude if you're not used to it. Soon, he tells her for example, we could play the bird identification game today, and then, shouting: I brought new recordings! The effect, she thinks, would be totally different if he said it the other way around: Soon, we could play the bird identification game today!, and then, whispering: I brought new recordings. And so, Soon learns not to try to read into what he says or how he says it, and she tries to focus only on the naked words and their immediate effects. As disconcerting as it may be, Old Man's weirdness, thinks Soon, is inoffensive; also disconcerting is the contrast between his face from the front and his face in profile—the former naive, even dopey, the latter introspective and wise, as if they were two different faces belonging to two different men.

He always wears the same suit, his fancy shoes, silk socks: it's clothing of excellent quality—even Soon, with her basic understanding of the matter, can see that. On recent days he's taken to putting a patterned handkerchief in his front jacket pocket, letting just a small triangle peek out, calculated, careful, and perfect. In spite of his dirty wrist and leg cuffs, Old Man clearly puts an effort into his attire and leaves nothing to chance. Now that it's gotten cooler he's also started wearing a coat; it's too big for him, dark brown, with an outdated cut. This coat has been with him for the past twenty years, he tells her. Here, feel it, he says, offering his sleeve. That's good cloth, they don't make it like that anymore!

Beside him, Soon knows she is not elegant. To her, clothes are just a way to cover up everything she doesn't like. She usually wears sports clothes a couple sizes too big. The changes in her body embarrass her, and she tries to hide them. She'd rather be a boy, she says. Boys aren't always on the alert about their anatomy, no one makes comments when they go by about whether their this-or-that has grown.

Although for her the worst thing is the attacks from other girls, her supposed friends—imposed by an adult conspiracy that forces them together—that cruel competition among girls to be the hottest. Soon has no problem talking about these matters with Old Man, although she's not about to admit her real hang-ups, which don't exactly have to do with growing, as she's told him, but with her plainness, the zits on her arms and her marshmallow body. She didn't know she was a marshmallow until last year, when Marga called her that in front of the other girls, and they all laughed spontaneously—without malice, so there was no point in getting mad; it was an affectionate comment, so the only possible reaction was to join in the laughter—to fake it—and then scrutinize herself in the mirror. What, exactly, does it mean to be a marshmallow? Marshmallow comes in many forms, as filling in candy bars or tiny cubes on hot chocolate. But she intuits that Marga is referring to her round face, soft and white, and her soft, plump body. Why does she feel so humiliated, so much so that she can't bring herself to tell anyone? Marga has nicknames for everyone, always related to food in some way, and no one seems to take them to heart as much as Soon: there's *Spaghetti*—Patri, who is frail; there's *Eggplant*—Lola, fat and dark; *Escarole*—Lidia, because of her short, curly hair; *Lentils*—David, the redhead; *Mini-Limes*—Lidia, with her tiny breasts; *Cuttlefish*—Rubén, tall and gawky. Why is *Marshmallow* worse, why does it hurt so bad?

Time without Old Man drags, the hours tense, so full of minutes, and each so similar to the next. But it's precisely the excess time that helps her differentiate nuances, observe that each moment has a specific light, a particular sound and even its own smell. There are constant changes, and they used to go unnoticed, seemingly tiny and insignificant, but now they are meaningful, even astonishing. Soon observes them meticulously, with real interest: the birth and destruction of an anthill, a new kind of insect that appears when it rains, the moss growing on the trunk of the Siberian elm—she now knows, because Old Man told her, what species it is—to extend upward like an outline on a map, transformations in the tonality and density of the grass, the variegation of the clouds and their rising speed, driven now by a colder, more constant wind. Sometimes she sinks deep into the contemplation of a tiny bit of earth, a microscopic ecosystem with minuscule fauna and minuscule flora, with hills and valleys, and she imagines herself living there, hiding there, protected and happy.

Things get worse when she starts to think about her life beyond the hedges, especially when she takes stock and finds that soon she'll have been skipping school for a full month. Ultimately, she knows that every change—the appearance or destruction of an anthill, every new bug or the growth of moss up the tree—is a mile marker on the road to the end. Then her stomach flip-flops, her palms start to sweat, her legs grow weak, and a strange tingling overtakes her feet.

Only Old Man can pull her out of that state, by talking to her or just being there.

Old Man also has his ups and downs, though most of the time he talks tirelessly, stringing together his stories about the behavior of birds—intelligent, artful, cunning, even twisted behavior . . . we mustn't idealize them! Shrikes, for example, are some great big liars. They fake calls of alarm so they can eat the food stores of other birds after they fly off in a fright. Another cheater is the cuckoo, which lays its eggs in another bird's nest so its chicks are fed by adoptive parents who don't notice the trick—even though the intruder can double them in size! If a fox approaches a whippoorwill's nest, the bird will fake a broken wing to catch the predator's attention and lure it away. And the hummingbird, so flashy, sweet, and colorful, is extremely promiscuous. They're all so crazy! Soon listens attentively, tries to extract the lesson that every story supposedly hides, because she's always been taught to interpret stories that way: casting the narrative aside to look for the moral it contains.

But Old Man doesn't always feel like talking. Lately he looks at her with a great deal of interest, as if she were turning into a new bird for him to study. Sometimes he falls silent and merely observes her with sad eyes and a yearning smile, as if he were searching for the right words to express something, words that in the end he never finds. Soon is unsettled when he gets like that. She thinks it's her fault for not interpreting his stories the right way. She feels awkward, uninteresting, boring. Still, he keeps visiting her every morning, and he stays longer every time—what started out as a few minutes, half an hour, is now an hour, or two, or three.

Clearly, Old Man is seeking something in her, even if Soon is incapable—at least for now—of giving it to him.

Don't you like any other animals, or other singers? Soon had asked her father if he knew who Nina Simone was, and he'd said yes, of course, though when it came to that era he preferred Aretha . . . Holliday or Billie . . . Franklin—she'd tried hard to memorize the names, but when she says them she knows she's gotten them wrong, and her voice trails off as she speaks. Anyway, if there are other singers just as good or even better, and lots of other animals in the world, why focus only on Nina Simone or only on birds? Old Man thinks for a few seconds before answering, only to finally admit that he doesn't know. He's always been like that, he says, stubborn and obsessive. If he likes a thing, he really likes it! And if you look at something—anything—up close, you always end up loving it. Soon is not very convinced by his argument. Some things, she says, looked at so closely, turn out to be awful. When she's put an insect, or even her own skin, under the microscope, what she saw was monstrous, straight out of a nightmare. She laughs when she says it, but Old Man isn't following the conversation now: he's gone quiet, tapping his fingers on a knee, with a slight tic at the corner of his mouth, as if he were trying to hold back a nervous laugh. After a bit he asks if she'd told her father about him. She rushes to reassure him: no, of course not, I just asked if he liked Nina Simone, that's all. It's true that her father was a little surprised at her knowledge, though. That she knew so many details about Nina's life, that is, because Soon had told him all she remembered. So she'd bluffed by saying she'd learned it all at school. And not only did he swallow her lie, but he was very pleased. Congratulate your music teacher for me, he'd said.

Old Man closes his eyes, rubs a thumb between his eyebrows. He starts to talk just like that, with his eyes still squeezed shut, forehead creased, his thumb moving up and down, and his voice rougher and more metallic than usual. Always, everyone, hides it, he says. Always, everyone, he repeats. Soon doesn't understand; she stammers out a question. Hides what? What is he talking about? Old Man's voice starts to rise: No one thinks about me, not ever! Everyone, always, is ashamed of me! *He* was the one who told her about Nina Simone's life, not some music teacher! Why is she leaving him out like everyone else does? Soon defends herself: Old Man, I couldn't tell my dad about you, or my mom either. They would never understand. Old Man's eyes widen, and they're damp now. What is it that your parents have to understand?, he asks. There's nothing strange about him, there's nothing bad! Isn't that right? Or does Soon, too, think he's bad and strange?

(It's not the first time Old Man has surprised her with this kind of outburst, free of any logic, although it is the first time he has let himself be swept up by that sad, desperate ferocity. That's how Old Man operates: he doesn't connect facts the way other people would, doesn't measure cause and effect in the same way. He considers things that would surprise others to be normal, and also the opposite, he's surprised by normal things. And yet, he is absolutely not dumb, thinks Soon: he knows so much information, so many details, he's so intelligent when it comes to useless things.)

It all started on a morning like any other. The alarm clock went off at the same time as always, and Soon lazed under the covers for a while, then dragged herself out of bed, washed her face, put on her track suit. When she went downstairs her parents were drinking coffee and talking in whispers; they went quiet when she entered the kitchen. She mixed a Cola Cao, nibbled on some madeleines. Same as always, says Soon, nothing to make her think that day would be different from any other. She didn't plan anything, had no way of knowing she was approaching the decisive moment, the moment when everything would change: she left the house and headed down the street, hurrying because she was a little late . . . and then she turned around. She turned around and sped up even more, but in the opposite direction. Not yet knowing what to do. Not knowing where she was headed. Not even knowing why or from what she was running. Her heart was pounding hard, but she felt strangely relieved, even happy. She sat down on a bench, took out some notebooks, pretended she was reading over them. After a while she got up, walked to another neighborhood and sat on another bench, spent another good while there, dissimulating. No one noticed her. Maybe she gave the impression she was older, maybe an underdeveloped sixteen—it happens: some girls develop late, they're slight and childish alongside their peers, girls among women. She spent the whole morning like that, wandering, until it was time to go home. She calculated the time exactly; her father opened the door for her, and his expression was the same as the day before, the week before: a routine, disinterested expression. They had lunch together. Her mother came home afterward, asked if she had much homework, if she wanted to go to the store later. Affectionate as always, both of them, not realizing a thing. She'd thought that her face would betray her, but no. Life went on the same whether she went to school or not. She knew then that she never wanted to go back.

But there was still the matter of her excuse. If she kept skipping, on the third day at the latest they would call her house to ask about her. That's how it always is: teachers chase the students down to make them go to class, even though at heart they'd rather the kids miss school, because it meant less work and calmer classrooms for them. Take Héctor, a repeating student who skipped school all the time, and who, when he did go, only caused trouble. Héctor didn't have the slightest interest in learning any of what was taught in those classrooms; he wanted to be a construction worker, but he had to wait until he was of legal age to leave school. He spent his time in class climbing on top of desks, throwing spitballs, and smacking his classmates on the back of the head, just out of boredom. Once, he went weeks without showing up, until an inspector came around and inquired about him and about the school's measures against his absenteeism. Absenteeism, kids, is punished, he told the other students there, the ones who never skipped, and his tone was very serious, menacing. Her case isn't comparable to

Héctor's because she is not under suspicion. From the outset she has a credibility that he would never have, since she has always been an obedient, disciplined, and even submissive girl, not at all rowdy—she would be terribly embarrassed, for example, to climb up onto a desk. But, even so, she had to give some explanation for her absence.

First she thought about calling in with a made-up excuse, then she considered faking a letter. She looked online and found some forms to request a school transfer. There were several kinds: she chose the SUT model (Sudden Urgent Transfer). If you thought about it, it really wasn't so strange: a sudden change in her parents' jobs or any other unforeseen event could force them to move, those things happen all the time, especially at the start of the year, right? She filled out the form, chose a random school in a nearby city as her transfer, included a fake phone number, and faxed it to her school from the copy shop near her house. So far, the trick was working. If anyone had called either of the schools to confirm the transfer or ask a question, Soon didn't know about it. Her parents were acting normal, she acted normal, life went on as normal: clearly, no one needed school.

It's because they hit you there, right? There? Where? At school, right? No, no, it's not that, says Soon, horrified. No? Your teachers don't hit you? When he was in school, it was normal to get the rod: smacks on the palm of your hand, tugs on the ear, and, for the most disobedient, a good swat. Even the most compassionate teachers did it: less often, but they did it. He remembers one who made a little elastic whip and attached a bag with a handful of garbanzos to the end. He was the one who took them to the gym, and if they fell off the pommel horse or didn't last long enough on the rings, he used his instrument to torment them while he called them faggots, homos, and queers. And it's true that he was a little effeminate, Old Man admits, with his flat feet and flutey voice, but oh, how it hurt! He laughs as he remembers, and the laugh consoles Soon, though she starts to fear that next to Old Man's memories, her own complaints sound insignificant.

No, no one hits her, she's never been hit, the problem is that they won't leave her alone. The only thing she wants, she insists, is to be left alone, but there's no hope of that. These days, all the teachers want to evaluate their students through group projects, but Soon doesn't feel comfortable working with anyone. When the kids break into groups she's inevitably left out, and the teacher has to intervene to keep her from being excluded. For her, it's worse to be forced into a group than to do the work alone. Her classmates look at her distrustfully just because she's been imposed on them. And Soon isn't one to be assertive and make herself useful, she just clams up, which doesn't help at all. She doesn't mind doing the assignments herself, she's never been lazy at schoolwork. She tells her teachers this—begs them, even—but they never listen, they insist she be part of the group, even if they have to force her. The groups always have one person who calls the shots, who manipulates the others just for the pleasure of dominating. Supposedly the teachers use these groups to promote equality—they use that expression: promote equality—but what they do is just the opposite: weaken the weak and strengthen the strong. It's not the same as getting hit, of course, but still . . .

Of course it's not the same, says Old Man. Her problem is worse! And he knows what he's talking about, he can compare! In the hospital where he stayed a while back they were also constantly forming groups. Reading groups, gardening groups, sports groups. And board game groups! They passed him from one to the other, and it never worked. They wanted to keep him entertained, but it all only depressed him. He just wanted to go out walking at night! You can walk, they told him, but only at authorized hours and only on authorized paths. But *everyone* was out walking on authorized paths at authorized hours, *all* the patients were there, forced to see and greet each other, and what he wanted was to walk alone. It was torture! Soon is at a loss for words as she listens. She doesn't know what hospital Old Man is referring to, what paths or what patients, until she dares to ask: were you sick? Old Man shrugs and replies: so they said!

Among birds, at least in some species, there are also dominant and dominated groups. It's not a decision they make freely: nature itself marks them when they're born—they come with different feathers! Needless to say it's the dominant birds who get the tastiest morsels and the healthiest females, who decide when to fly and to where the flock must follow them. There was one experiment where some scientists wondered what would happen if they camouflaged the weakest, made them pass for dominant. They dyed their feathers to disguise them! But it didn't work at all. The very attitude of the fakers gave them away; it wasn't a matter of plumage, but of demeanor.

With her eyes half-closed, Soon tries to extract the lesson of the story. Does he mean the two of them are like dyed birds? But now Old Man is talking about another kind of bird: the ones that refused to take part in the game. They were hardly mentioned in the writeup of results, but there were some specimens—not many, but some!—that were discarded as useless. I had to find the information in the article's footnotes, so unimportant were these rebels considered! But why were they useless?, asks Soon. Because when they were disguised they died of sadness, they refused to eat or fly, they didn't even try to fake it! They didn't *want* to be in any group, and if they were forced to, they kept apart, even if it meant rejection. Surviving with a disguise, for those birds, meant a slow death; that's why they chose to speed up their deaths, without any trickery.

Old Man always has a backpack with him. He opens it to show Soon what it holds: the binoculars, his bird books, clippings from magazines and newspapers, a pencil case—he likes pencils, not pens—the towel for sitting on the grass, a notebook, his cellphone and headphones. It's an old backpack, light green, with tattered brown straps; it's like what a soldier would carry, or an explorer. Soon's backpack is brand-name, with bright colors and zippers, waterproof. Does Old Man expect her to show him what's inside hers, too? The thought makes her ashamed, she realizes how childish everything she keeps in it is—if only she at least had a pack of tobacco, a lighter, or a bracelet from a night-club. Not even her cellphone—she's not allowed to take it to school with her—not even that. Just text books, a binder with florescent dividers, also a pencil case—though hers holds gel pens of every color—shreds of foil, napkins, sunflower seed shells. Soon is messy, while Old Man is methodical and organized. Would you like to keep the towel?, he offers, and she shakes her head hard. No, no, I'd lose it, she says. But didn't they already have this conversation? Old Man repeats himself, the words mix together, it's all confused, she's lost count of the days.

He lives nearby, he says, about five minutes away on foot, in a ten-floor apartment building—he's on the eighth. It has a little kitchen, a living room without a TV, a bathroom with a commode that always gets clogged, a bedroom with a single bed, another bedroom where he stores boxes of his things. What things?, asks Soon, and he explains diffidently, as if it were all too obvious. His magazines! His albums! His ste-reo equipment! The notebooks with his notes! Some of his mother's clothes! Dishes, saucepans that he still hasn't used but that people insisted on giving him! And what's Soon's apartment like? What floor is she on? That's the typical landscape in the area: apartments in tall buildings, brown towers, green towers, small windows, little balconies that recall drinking troughs in canary cages. Soon shakes her head. No, no, she lives in a house, she's already explained; a few years ago they moved to a house, and that was right when everything started to go wrong for them—or for her, because her brother, after all, had left. The house has two yards, one in front and the other in back, and a storage shed—it's big, there's always more to clean. The whole street is full of houses just like it; some people park their cars in front, others don't, and that's the only difference. But those houses . . . where are they? I haven't seen any houses like that around here! Of course not, Soon tells him, because they're not here; it takes her over half an hour to walk to the park, doesn't he remember? Old Man closes his eyes, reflects. Houses are worse, he says, because they don't have views, he prefers the view he has from his apartment—I can see the expressway, miles and miles of expressway! At night it's a show worth watching because the car headlights shine, lines and lines of cars that go one direction and the other, it's crazy! Some want to go one direction and others in exactly the opposite direction, and they get stuck, they always get stuck. Someday Soon should come to his place to see the expressway from so high up, she'd be surprised how pretty it is, she can't imagine. Yes, she should come, he repeats, he'd be delighted to show her. In the building's eaves there are also some swallows' nests, and with any luck you can see them peeking their heads out—another show! Old Man makes his suggestion calmly, without changing his tone of voice, as if he weren't really saying it seriously or there weren't anything malicious behind it, and because of that Soon doesn't let it trouble her, or not too much.

She started to feel bad when her brother left. Her brother said he loved her, but it wasn't true, because he left unapologetically, claiming that he had to go. Had to? That's what makes Soon the angriest: that he would disguise his freely made decision as an obligation. Is a person forced to do a master's degree? That's the first thing. And, in second place, why did he insist on studying abroad? Weren't any of the programs in his hometown good enough for him? Or did he do it to escape, to get away from her? Of course, Soon had begged him to stay. She'd begged him in tears, she'd pleaded, but in vain. He looked at her with sorrow, he wrung his hands, assured her he also felt bad about leaving, very bad, and he said he was sorry, but his words—the words *bad* or *sorry*, for example—sounded so false they tore into her. Her brother is older, nine years older than her, and it's been ten months since he left. Soon often goes into his room, still full of his clothes and books, to remember him more intensely, though it makes her even sadder.

Old Man listens attentively, nodding to show he understands her. Between them is a bag of Cheetos, which they casually share. She pauses to lick her fingers, blows a lock of hair off her forehead instead of touching it with greasy fingers. Her parents are older, she says, that's why there are so many years between her and her brother. One time, Marga insinuated that she must have been one of those kids who

43

are born by accident. Your parents made a mistake, she said, and you came by surprise. Marga was trying to upset her, but the truth is that being an unwanted baby fits perfectly with Soon's vision of herself—I've always felt like I came from a different world, she says. Although in the end it wasn't true that she was unwanted. She got up the nerve to ask her mother, who denied it roundly. She'd been wanted, very wanted, her mother insisted. Though I guess that's no guarantee of anything, she concludes, scooping out the last Cheeto crumbs.

Physically, she doesn't resemble anyone, which makes her happy. She is horrified by those daughters who are identical to their mothers: it's already clear just how they're going to deteriorate over time. Though she is full of hang-ups, at least she doesn't know how she will evolve, and sometimes she allows herself to dream up her own version of the story of the ugly duckling, in which she eventually becomes a lovely, alluring girl. Mysterious. Old Man has told her that her eyes are pretty, dreamy. *Dreamy* is a word that she finds interesting, even if she doesn't know exactly what her friend is referring to. Like squinty?, she asks, like I was a little sleepy? Old Man smiles and says no: That would be more like *drowsy*!

(Old Man has a large vocabulary, she can tell he's read a ton, though he won't admit it and claims to read only magazines about birds. Well, he concedes, it could also be because he listens to the radio—every night, he listens to a call-in program where lonely people talk about their lives just so they can be heard. The program has existed for several decades, and there's never any shortage of people who call in; there are always peculiar lives to tell, really strange lives that are also full of very strange words.)

Physically, Soon repeats, she doesn't resemble anyone, not her father—who is tall and thin—or her mother—who is very blonde and has fine eyebrows and a much smaller mouth—and of course not her brother—who has a square face and freckles like their father. Oddly, the three of them share a certain bearing; you can tell they're from the same family even though they don't exactly have the same features. But Soon isn't like them at all, she says, and when she says it she smiles with pride: lately, she's pleased to feel different, and she doesn't care that different could mean worse.

And him? Does he take after his parents? Old Man gives her a long, watery look; he shrugs his shoulders. What a question, he says: if he resembles his father, he also resembles his mother. He takes after them both, he adds: it's inevitable! Soon doesn't understand why his reply is accompanied by that contorted expression, that pained melancholy. Maybe he misses his parents. Maybe his parents died a long time ago, maybe in an accident that he still hasn't gotten over. When it comes to his family, Soon knows practically nothing, but it's hard to ask when he reacts like that, ducking the question. Faced with the slightest pang of discomfort or pain, Old Man always changes the subject.

(There's very little that Soon knows about Old Man's life. So far: that he was beaten at school as a child, that he spent time in a hospital, that he lives alone on the eighth floor, that he's worn the same coat for twenty years, that he doesn't pay taxes because he doesn't work, that he's afraid—though less and less!—of being annoying, that he prefers pencils to pens, that he listens to call-in confessions at night on the radio. Things like that, incidental tidbits that he tells her unexpectedly and out of order. When he talks about subjects he knows about he's didactic, organized, and repetitive, but when he talks about his own life—or mentions it, as if in passing—he does it in a quiet voice, with sentences that trail off and things left unspoken, as if there were no need to explain further.)

By now she is a semi-expert on birds. What at first had seemed useless and boring—learn their scientific names! recognize their songs!—has now become entertaining, even a mark of distinction and superiority: she is convinced that no one—no one!—her age knows as much in this field as her. What if someday she became an ornithologist? What if she traveled to the jungle to study tropical birds, and on one of her expeditions she discovered a new species, an extraordinarily beautiful one that no human being had ever seen before? Only Old Man can listen to her delusions of grandeur without laughing. Quite the opposite: he listens with passion and pride. He's getting on in years, but if he could, he would go to the jungle with her! They would make a great team!

He gives her a poster of songbirds: goldfinch, linnet, greenfinch, serin . . . Soon now recognizes them easily, knows what they look like and how they behave. I'll hang it up in my room, she tells him, and she's grateful but doesn't kiss his cheek, because she feels there is something inappropriate about it: not just the kiss, but the very act of the gift, even in hanging his gift in her room—in bringing Old Man, that way, into her room. Her father, seeing her so enthusiastic about her new obsession, has started calling her *featherbrain*, though in an affectionate way. He also teases her by saying her new hobby is *for the birds,* but she doesn't care, it's not like that's a bad thing. But Old Man doesn't like those expressions at all. There's something slippery and malicious in those sayings and refrains: figures of speech confuse him, he never catches on! For a long time people tortured him with those kinds of maxims: *the early bird catches the worm* or *kill two birds with one stone,* what a pain! (Soon understands what he means. She feels the same way when people call her *marshmallow,* though she will never admit it.)

They almost miss each other. When Old Man arrives, the maintenance workers are cutting the grass and trimming the shrubs with a great racket: very large tools for such a small thing, Old Man says later, when he comes back and finds her sitting in the usual spot. They've just left, right?, he asks, and she nods, patting the newly cut grass, see this?, she says, and also those—pointing to the hedges—before, the branches stuck out every which way, and now they're perfect, too neat, all nice and square, she says with a grimace of distaste; it's so clean it even smells different. Old Man sniffs. I think they fumigated, he says, and then he asks what she did while the maintenance workers worked, where she went to wait them out. She sighs and tells the truth: first she prowled around the pond, looking at the fish, but then she decided to leave the park, and she crossed the avenue to the outpatient clinic, and that's where she waited, sitting and killing time. Not inside the clinic—where she might attract attention waiting alone—but outside, on one of the benches under a portico with a ramp for mothers with baby carriages and patients in wheelchairs.

What she doesn't tell him is how horrible a time she had putting up that front, trying not to stand out as she sat there alone with her school backpack and her almost-fourteen years. A pale blonde woman sat down on the bench and didn't take her eyes off her, until she got a phone call and forgot Soon. Then a nurse came out to smoke, a young male nurse with a tattoo on his arm, and he stared at her too. She still feels ashamed from that look. She stretched out her shirt to cover herself as much as possible and even moved a little away from the portico, but she could still feel those eyes boring into her body. The nurse stayed there a good while, until finally a female nurse came out whom he'd clearly arranged to meet. He grabbed her by the waist, pinched her ass, and whispered something into her ear; she laughed and walked off, shimmying her hips with happiness. Soon felt so much like crying that she had to lock herself in the bathroom and let the tears flow. She cried without understanding why she was uncomfortable: if only she hadn't seen that nurse, and especially not the two nurses together, with their private jokes and secrets. As she recalls it now her eyes well up again, but Old Man is utterly oblivious. He's taking out a guidebook on Anatidae, you haven't seen this one, he tells her, and she tries to take an interest in its pages, her nose still stinging and her eyes tearing up, although maybe, she thinks, it's mostly a reaction to the newly cut grass, or to the chemical fumigation.

Look, Soon, Old Man says, and he shows her an old photograph of him when he was younger, in his early twenties. He has an enormous parrot perched on his arm, and the colors of its feathers are washed out by the poor quality of the image, but they're still beautiful, spectacular even. That's Ruper, he explains, he belonged to a neighbor. Old Man is against imprisoning animals in cages, especially tropical species, but Ruper was fascinating and Old Man had observed him every day, studied his behavior, and that way he'd learned a ton more things about birds; Old Man, like Soon, believes in the virtues of auto-didacticism—why go to school just so someone can tell you what's in a book? Isn't it better to disengage, move to one side, and watch? She looks at the man in the photo, older than her, much older, but undeniably younger than the one she has in front of her now, and of course handsomer, surprisingly handsome. In the photo, Old Man's damp hair is combed back into a pompadour like an old-timey film actor, and he has high cheekbones, a smooth forehead, and very white teeth, nice and new. He's wearing a jacket and a bow tie; you can't see what he's wearing on the bottom because the photo cuts off at his waist. Old Man looks at the camera and smiles; he's happy. What is it that's happened to him since then, aside from time? A lot of girls must have liked him, Soon has no doubt about that now. Why didn't he marry any of them? Why didn't he have kids? Old Man has never talked about women or children, so Soon presumes he has always been alone. Although, if she thinks about it, why should she assume that? Maybe she should change her conception of things. Maybe Old Man has had a lot of girlfriends, maybe he still does, maybe he's fathered children left and right, maybe he's keeping secrets every bit as elegant and decadent as the pompadour he had when he was young. It's hard to believe when she looks at him now, with his frayed suit and crazy hair, but not when she looks at that photo, which reveals countless other possibilities: a whole entire past.

At first she thinks she's peed herself on accident, but when she realizes where the wetness is coming from, she's scared, doesn't know what to do, her hands start to shake and she feels hot. What she finds when she pulls down her pants is a color more brown than red, a substance much thicker than blood, nastier than blood, though she's heard that this is just the beginning, that later on come spurts of real blood, liters and liters of blood that are impossible to hide, and it goes on for days. What to do now? Wait for Old Man and tell him? Ask him—him!—to bring her some cloth or a pad? Act like nothing is wrong, while the blood soaks through her clothes? She stuffs in some Kleenex as best she can and waits in distress.

It had to happen, but maybe not this way, not like this.

She was one of the last in her class; it took so long she had to pretend she'd gotten it to avoid backhanded comments. Lesbos don't have periods, did you guys know that?, Marga had said, and all the girls nodded, giggling: of course, that's why they can't have kids . . . The day her mother tried to talk to her about the subject, Soon flatly refused: I don't need it, I don't need it!, she shouted, offended. But she did need it, though it's a little late to admit that now.

How long will she be like this? How long is normal? Could she die of blood loss if it doesn't stop? Will the stains be obvious? What if it hurts? Can she complain, or is it better to keep quiet? What is she expected to do? What do others do?

When he arrives, Old Man looks at her worriedly. What's wrong?, he asks, you don't look so good. Soon bursts into tears. He crouches down beside her. She can tell him whatever it is, he says, he knows how to keep secrets, and plus, he'll try to help her! But Soon feels resentful as she listens. Of course she can't tell him. Supposedly this is an important day in the life of every girl, the day when a new phase begins—the day she becomes a woman!—but she feels more like everything is ending, and the last ties she had to the outside world have now been definitively broken. A woman? If this is what being a woman is, she doesn't want to be one. Old Man is still there, kneeling down, thoughtful. You're not going to tell me?, he asks. You don't trust me? His voice rises from one question to the next, and Soon remembers his fits of fury when he feels left out. She's afraid of offending him again—he changes so much when he's upset—but this time she doesn't know how to avoid it. Old Man, don't get mad, it's women's stuff. Women's stuff?, repeats Old Man, and his incipient indignation transforms into curiosity. What do you mean, women's stuff? Menstruation, Soon explains, immediately feeling ridiculous—why did she use that word, so cold and clinical? Old Man looks at her in astonishment, until he understands and turns red like a light bulb. I don't know what you're talking about!, he says then, and he ducks his head as he starts to take things out of his backpack, announcing them aloud as he sets them on the grass: towel!, binoculars!, cheese puffs!, the Nina Simone biography by David Brun-Lambert! This book has a ton of mistakes!, he says, shaking it. Let me tell you!

But he doesn't. That day he leaves early, and Soon leaves too. After all, it's not unusual, the teachers let some girls go home early their first time, no questions asked. Luckily, she's saved herself the sarcastic teasing and giggles from Marga and the other girls: they would have unmasked the novice. Much better, no doubt about it, to face Old Man's reaction: an ostrich hiding its head, but at least he doesn't tease her.

How can it be that he doesn't work, when he knows so much? Sure, he's old—that's why she calls him that, Old Man, and it's no insult—but he hasn't reached retirement age, so, unless he's won the lottery—and Soon doesn't think he has—she is looking at an untapped talent. David Attenborough is much much older, an elderly man by now, and he still appears on TV in his documentaries, so couldn't Old Man make documentaries too, or report stories, or write bird guidebooks? Soon is gloomy, she still doesn't understand the purpose of bleeding every month—for her, it's one more sign of the world's absurdity. What a waste, she thinks, and her mood has infected the conversation, which she approaches gently today, with a confidential and melancholic tone. Old Man moves a little closer and sighs. Why doesn't he work? Well, there aren't many places where he feels comfortable, he must admit. He doesn't understand why, but most places turn him away. He doesn't have formal studies, that's a fact, but even at places where they aren't required, after the interview, he is always sent away. He hasn't aspired to anything for a long time now. Why make a fuss, it's better to stay home or walk in the park, doesn't she agree? He does miss the days when he used to work at a wild bird sanctuary, it's true. There was no salary, but it was payment enough that they let him be there, surrounded by birds. The cages were just for the sick ones or for the babies born in captivity—otherwise they were totally free! It was an aquatic reserve that recovered species in danger of extinction, and he was part of that accomplishment, how could he not feel proud! Perking up a bit, Soon asks him to tell her more—what did he do, exactly? Well, he helped out wherever he could, in all kinds of tasks, from cleaning excrement out of the cages and sweeping up dry leaves to putting out the birdseed and regulating the thermostat in the chicks' cages. He's not too proud to get his hands dirty! He can be a tough guy when he wants! His eyes turn introspective and he says: I loved being there, it was wonderful to watch the birds in their ponds, the red-crested pochards and the flamingos and also the yellow-billed oxpeckers, the western swamphens, the glossy ibis, and the storks. There were a lot of birds that came through the place, but some of them he recognized perfectly well, and he named them after singers, regardless of whether they were male or female: Aretha, Roberta, Billie, Diana, Linda, and of course Nina, who was a blue crane—also called a paradise crane—with a slow and majestic walk. He also managed to make friends! The other volunteers were lovely, kind people who treated him well. Especially the keeper, a woman he accompanied in all her chores—he became her shadow, all with the goal of helping her! And what happened, Old Man? Why didn't you keep working there?, asks Soon, hugging her knees. He opens his eyes wide as if waking up to another world—the world of the hideout and scarce water—and he looks down at his hands and explains: nothing, the program came to an end, that's all. His change in attitude and his sadness are so obvious that Soon can anticipate what will happen next: Old Man will get up, put away his towel, talk about something else as a cover, then say goodbye and walk hurriedly away. That's

what always happens when something makes him uncomfortable. This time it's fine with Soon because she needs to
leave too, needs to make a stop at the clinic bathroom, a
quick trip because she hates that place—the clinic. Now that
she's a woman, though, she can't be picky, she needs to have
bathrooms nearby where she can wash up—just one more
disadvantage to being a woman, no doubt about that.

It's strange that it hadn't rained sooner: they went practically
all of October without a single drop, and now, suddenly, a
streak of downpours. What bad luck, they say to each other,
looking worriedly at their hideout, now a muddy pit. Old
Man showed up with filthy shoes and the hems of his pants a
disaster. Soon is wearing her raincoat and boots, but even so
they obviously can't stay there. Rainy days are now lost days,
and it's better to go somewhere else than to lurk nearby—
better than going back, again, to the clinic. But they leave
separately; they can't show themselves in public together,
and for Soon it would even be weird to see Old Man beyond
the shrubs, to see him inside the world she's trying to
escape. She decides on a downtown library full of university students. Next to them she is clearly much younger, but
the rooms are so jam-packed that no one stops to look at
her longer than two seconds, such is her insignificance, her
lack of importance in that alien world of adults. She could
arrange to meet Old Man there, in the library, but then she
would risk her invisibility; together, they would inevitably
draw attention: her, a child, and him, an old man. Imagining

it—not that they met up at the library, but that people noticed them and speculated on their relationship—produces a strange thrill in her—the thrill of transgression—and she often dreams up scenarios that include a police intervention, Old Man's arrest, an interrogation full of questions with hazy sexual connotations under a ruthless spotlight. But it's one thing to imagine, and quite another to play with fire. She'd be terrified if something like that happened in real life. So what she does when it rains—or when the day threatens rain—is spend the morning alone in the library, writing—she has to entertain herself somehow—a kind of diary where she imagines scenes that could be, that she wishes would happen—but no, but no—scenes that at the end of the day she tears up in embarrassment. Meanwhile, Old Man is surely going other places, more places where she shouldn't meet up with him, like bars or stores or markets—Soon doesn't know about that, what Old Man does when he isn't with her.

Of course she's heard about the maniacs who pursue children. People are forever telling stories about men who kidnap kids on their way out of school and do bad things to them, even torture and kill them. There'd been one boy from a nearby neighborhood who disappeared, and no one knew anything more about him until two years later, when they found his bones buried in a vacant lot. Soon's parents made sure to lower their voices when they talked about it, but there was no point in that, the story would reach her ears somehow. The autopsy—as Soon heard on her neighbors' TV—revealed that the boy had been raped before and after his death. That expression, *before and after his death*, shocked her even more than the fact of the rape itself, since she wasn't very clear on what it meant to be raped, and her knowledge was so blurry that she could allow herself to ignore it. But that a maniac was doing horrible things to a boy *before and after his death* spoke clearly of a death, a death for which that maniac had been present and from which he hadn't run: death as part of the process. The day Soon heard the autopsy details she was wearing a red summer dress, too childish for her age, too short, with absurd, ruffled sleeves. From that day on she refused to wear it again; her mother never understood why, and she'd only given up because Soon was—could sometimes be—very stubborn. Soon wouldn't admit the real reason for her aversion, because not even she understood it. She only had to see the dress hanging in her closet and she felt a murky unease, and she knew full well it was irrational, but there it was, marking a change.

Still, it was all just words and symbols, even that incident, since she had never seen a maniac up close. That's what she called them, maniacs, though lately she had also heard people talk about *pedophiles*, which must mean more or less the same thing. *Depraved* was a word that for a long time she'd confused with *depressed*, and she didn't know if it had to do with children exclusively, or just with anything of a sexual nature. Like all kids, she had been educated in the suspicion of strangers: don't talk to them, don't accept gifts from them, absolutely don't trust them, etc. But Soon will be fourteen soon, and the rules of the game are starting to change. If she never talked to strangers, she thinks, she'd never get any-where. An acquaintance was once a stranger, that's the way of things, no matter what: if we went through life refusing to speak to anyone we didn't know, we would never meet anyone. People were always insisting she should have more friends, that it was good to interact with others and bad to spend all day shut up in her house. They forced her to do group projects with people she didn't know anything about, except that they were her age and went to the same school. Just because of that, they're not strangers? When does a stranger achieve the category of potential friend, and when does he stay, merely, a potential danger? Clearly, Old Man doesn't fit in the category of friends that her environment wants her to have; rather, he's dangerously close to the cat-egory of maniac or pedophile, but only because of his age and the fact that he doesn't go to her school. Otherwise, she doesn't see how he could be suspicious. He has never tried to kidnap her; he's never even laid a hand on her.

When she was in grade school, three or four years ago, a psychologist came to give a talk about sexual abuse. She told the students they should always tell their parents or teachers if an adult ever touched them in a strange way. At the question of what counted as *strange*, she gave several examples: a hand between the legs, on the knee or the thigh. One boy raised his hand with a question. He explained that his English teacher would sometimes grab his neck, but as a joke. When he was asked to give more details, the boy said his teacher would grab him from behind, at the nape of the neck, and squeeze him there for a while so he couldn't get away, as a joke, he repeated. But did he move his hand?, asked the psychologist, and also: how long did he stay like that, holding him? Five minutes, said the boy—though he probably didn't really know how long five minutes was. Like this long, he said, and then he staged the scene with his friend, both of them rolling with laughter. The psychologist said that she would have a talk with the English teacher, just in case. That bit about the nape of the neck is the only thing Soon remembers about the presentation.

In any case, Old Man has never touched the nape of her neck, either.

He knows he's not allowed to talk to children—some policemen warned him about that once—but luckily Soon is no longer a child, so there shouldn't be a problem, right?, and he furrows his brow. What policemen warned him, and why?, she wants to know. Oh, it happened a long time ago, he says. He didn't know it was forbidden! That's what he told the police, too—that he'd never seen it written anywhere that you couldn't talk to children. The scene was this: Old Man was taking his morning walk one very hot day. He stopped to rest beside a school; on the playground, some small children were playing—they were maybe six or seven years old! He thought they were really funny because they didn't mind at all about being out under that beating sun, they were immune to the blistering heat. They were jumping, throwing water balloons at each other, and clowning around, while the teacher who was supposedly watching them fanned herself on the sidelines, in the shade. Old Man went up to the fence and called them over with a *psst!* so he could talk to them. First came one, more daring than the rest, and then came the others—one by one!—shaking off their shyness and giggling. Old Man said to them: throw one of those water balloons at me, too, I'm dying in this heat, I want a water bomb, and the boys threw it at him, rolling with laughter. He sat down on the ground so he could keep talking to them. To get down to their level, he explains, because they really were very small! That was when he saw his neighbor walk past on the opposite sidewalk, and she stared at him in astonishment, although at the moment he didn't think it was important, he just raised his hand to wave at her and then stayed there with the kids a while longer. They talked about how much water you can get into a balloon before it explodes, and about how the color of the rubber gets lighter as it swells. He told them how something similar happens to a bird's belly when it stuffs itself with food, but, unlike balloons, bellies never explode. He was so absorbed in the conversation that he didn't hear the policemen arrive, he only realized it because of the expressions on the boys' faces!, and then he turned his head and there they were, two policemen, one young and the other older, both very serious, very professional. What are you doing here?, they asked him. I was talking to the kids, he said. You don't talk to children, said the younger policeman, while the older one shooed them all away, let's go, go on, get out of here, and they scattered like frightened little chicks, fear spreading from one to the other. Someone must have also told the teacher, because she came running over now all alarmed, exaggeratedly alarmed, almost shouting, my god, my god, she was saying, how awful, it's horrible, my children, my children, what have you done to my babies?, when the truly horrible thing—says Old Man—was the opportunism of that teacher who hadn't cared a bit about the kids until the police came! My babies, my babies, she cried, and even the older policeman seemed embarrassed when he soothed her: don't worry, ma'am, they were just talking. But the other policeman, the younger one, was much more severe, his eyes were like steel—like two steel marbles—and his lips very thin and tense, and he said: talking to children is not permitted, do you understand me, sir? He also asked why Old Man had those binoculars with him, what he was planning to look at. Birds, said Old Man. Birds!, repeated the policeman contemptuously. We don't want to see you here ever again, not you and not your binoculars, the next time we'll have to bring you in for questioning. Questioning?, Old Man asked, intrigued. He could answer those questions now, no problem, it was no trouble if it would save them time and make their job easier, but they must have taken his offer as a provocation. The younger cop, furious, stepped up to Old Man threateningly and said: did you not understand me, sir, or are you playing dumb? The other cop, the older one, tried to calm him down and told him to leave Old Man alone. He's a fruitcake, poor guy, can't you see that?, he said. This hurt Old Man much more than the scolding: that this cop, who was clearly nicer and more understanding than the other, classified him as a *fruitcake*. But it hurt even more to learn—as he did later—that it was his neighbor who had called the police, the neighbor who had seen him from across the street, his neighbor whom he'd known for years and said hello to and wished a merry Christmas, whom he helped with her bags when she was overloaded, to whom he'd given a wooden birdhouse as a gift, and who he'd always thought liked him, though from that day onward he knew she didn't, how disappointing!

The rat is prowling serenely around the foot of the tree when Soon slips through the hole in the shrubs. It lifts its head and looks at her, unfazed, until she screams, and then—only then—it scurries away, though listlessly. Soon's scream was more from surprise than disgust. The rat wasn't totally ugly; it looked kind of cute when it turned its head, with its little nose trembling and its dazed and myopic eyes. Even so, she wouldn't like for it to come back. She's always heard that rats spread disease, and that when they're cornered, they turn aggressive and jump up to bite your face. Soon would not like to be bitten in the face. She already looks ugly enough, and can't afford to be disfigured by a rat bite. It occurs to her that she could buy poison and put it in the hideout. But when she suggests this to Old Man, he starts waving his arms wildly, aghast. Absolutely not!, he says. Poison could get eaten by dogs, by birds, any little animal that comes by. Even just thinking about the rats: does she really want to give them such a horrible death? They're no threat, they run away when someone approaches them! She immediately feels ashamed, and pretends she'd only said it as a joke. Old

Man repeats, very seriously: that's right, no poison here. Poison is forbidden! It's forbidden even to think about poison!

(Only later will Soon find out that he once took poison. Not really to kill himself, he admits, he just did it to get attention, out of desperation, even knowing he ran the risk of dying. All he wanted to do was show the people at the clinic that he really did need to go out alone. If they let him walk alone, even if only for a little while—at night, for example, when there was no chance of meeting anyone—he would get well much sooner. He'd recover in no time! But his strategy had the opposite effect. They didn't understand a thing. They didn't leave him alone for a minute. They gave him new medicines, some drops that made him drowsy all day long and some very painful injections that got him smiling like a dummy. He realized that these people, the mind police, would only leave him alone when he followed all the rules one by one: schedules, doses, taking turns, group activities, teamwork, etc. He changed his tactics and was out of there in a year.

But all of this, for the moment, Soon does not know.)

Does she know that type of bird that doesn't have feet, and since it can't land anywhere, spends its whole life in the air? Propped on one elbow, Soon looks at him incredulously. That's impossible, she says, there's no such thing as birds without feet. Yes, there is, insists Old Man, I saw one once! Really, I saw a dead one! It had fallen to the ground, exhausted, and it was light blue, and its body was as small as a pinky finger. It weighed less than a feather, but its wings spread out were very wide, and so transparent you could see the color of the sky through them. That's what's called protection coloring, he explains. Camouflage. That way they protect themselves from hawks or other predators, for example, but it also keeps us from seeing them! These birds, Old Man goes on, do everything in the air, they spend their whole lives up there, they eat and sleep in the wind, and they only come down to the ground to die! I'd like to live like that, murmurs Soon. Old Man smiles. He would too, there are a lot of people who dream of being those birds, always flying and flying and never getting dirty on the ground. Uncorrupted, he adds, thoughtful.

They are both silent as they look at the sky, scrutinizing it. She asks for the binoculars and amuses herself with them for a good while. If he ever finds the body of another legless bird, she says, could he pick it up so he can show it to her? It's not that she doesn't trust him, it's just really hard for her to imagine that a creature like that exists, and she would give anything to see it. If only it were possible to be so free, she thinks, to fly without touching the ground, but the truth is that all birds have legs and Old Man's story must be a legend or a myth. Soon doesn't believe in legends and myths, although she doesn't say this to Old Man: she doesn't want to make him mad or offend him.

One thing is for sure: Soon's musical tastes have changed. Old Man catches her softly singing *Why don't you see it? Why don't you feel it? I don't know, I don't know. You don't have to live next to me, just give me my equality,* and he interrupts her: Soon, do you know what you're singing? She has no idea; she was singing to herself without thinking. "Mississippi Goddam," one of Nina Simone's legendary songs! She composed it in only an hour! It was one of her first protest songs! Those aren't the only lyrics Soon has learned inadvertently, and that's in spite of the fact that she's not very good at English. Old Man isn't either, but he's memorized all Nina's songs in all their versions, plus where they come from, who composed them and on what date, their translations and meanings, their histories and anecdotes, where Nina sang them for the first time, where the last. Of course, he's collected the complete discography of his goddess, including rarities and vinyl, even though he doesn't have a record player.

For Soon, it's still a mystery where he gets his money, though it's clear he doesn't have much, and that he spends the little he does have almost exclusively on his hobbies. She has the impression that the only thing he eats is the junk food he shares with her, and buns dipped in *cafe con leche*. He's told her himself that he buys three buns a day: one for the birds and two for him. Two buns a day, the junk food, and maybe a banana—it's the only fruit he allows himself, he says: the cheapest, pure phosphorus! That must be his basic diet. When Soon unwraps her sandwich and the smell of cold cuts wafts out, he just watches in silence. Soon usually offers him a bite and he always refuses, but she thinks that's just a show of refinement, and he's really dying for a taste.

One morning he shows up dressed differently, without his suit, in jeans that are too big for him and a green and orange striped long-sleeved polo shirt. He exudes an air of abandonment; it's clear he isn't comfortable, that he even feels ashamed. He's wearing a leather belt just to keep his pants from falling down, and it forms a lot of pleats around the belt loops. It looks like a head of lettuce, thinks Soon, but she pretends not to notice. She needn't bother. Old Man himself, aggrieved, brings up his appearance. He had to bring his suit to the cleaners, and the only thing he has are these clothes, which were given to him. Soon asks who gave them to him, and she also asks him why he only has one suit. He has two, Old Man says, puffing out his chest, a winter one and a summer one! They're good suits, they cost over five hundred euros each when he bought them, and that was many years ago now. He also has several shirts, four or five, and some ties, although those are only for special occasions! Since they are good clothes, unsuited to the washing machine, he brings them to the cleaners when he needs to. He brings everything at once, because they give you a discount the more articles of clothing you bring, and that's why he's left with nothing now! As for the clothes he's wearing—those awful jeans and the striped shirt—they belonged to a friend of his at the clinic, and when his friend died they gave the clothes to Old Man, wrapped in a bundle with other belongings. His friend didn't die, he says then: he hung himself. He's wearing the clothes of a hanged man!

He feels truly sad today and isn't worried about sparing Soon his pain. His friend killed himself, he repeats, and now he uses his friend's clothes when he has nothing to wear. In the past, when he brought his clothes to the cleaners, he didn't leave the house until he got the call letting him know he could pick them up. You can't go out in public looking like this, he says; no man should ever wear jeans! But things are different now. I can't miss seeing you just because of this, right?, he says, pointing to his clothes. No, of course not, replies Soon, though it's true that she prefers him in his suit: in a suit, he's a distinguished and even mysterious old man, a man of decadent elegance. Like this, he just looks like a poor old man, almost a bum.

Soon never liked to go to school. When she was little, her father rewarded her with candy if she walked the whole way there without complaining. If she also smiled and looked happy—that is, if she faked it—she could get two candies. Candy as bait: she liked the lemon ones with a soft filling, sweet but also slightly tangy. They were big and you sucked on them for several minutes until your tongue filled, suddenly, with an explosion of flavor and a strange, viscous effervescence. Her mother said they weren't healthy—too much sugar in that candy!—and that's why her father gave them to her on the sly, though now she thinks all that secrecy was something the two of them planned to make it more exciting—extra motivation for Soon. But what happened was that she ended up despising those candies. She associated their taste with the forced walk, with the kids standing on corners with backpacks, waiting for each other, looking at her from above or below, never head on. She especially hated having to walk past a group of kids. She still hates that.

Last year she'd had a look at the guidance counselor's notebook. The woman had called Soon into her office to talk about her integration problems—Soon never would have diagnosed herself that way, with *integration problems*—but she had to step out for a moment to make a private telephone call—*a private telephone call,* she'd said: the guidance counselor talked like that all the time. Soon sat waiting in her chair with the assessment notebook in front of her, facing the other way, open to her page. Afraid she would be caught, she strained to read it without moving, deciphering the letters upside down, which wasn't an easy task. And what did it say?, asks Old Man, also intrigued. *Integration problems,* replies Soon, those two words were underlined in red. And also: *maladjusted but intelligent, possibly believes herself superior to her peers.* This surprised her a lot, because what Soon feels is somehow *inferior,* not *superior* to others, and she's offended that the guidance counselor, who hasn't spoken to her for even a single minute, would write precisely the opposite. There were also some notes on her family. *Structured,* it said. *Older parents. Liberal professions. Second child. Good neighborhood.* She couldn't help but reach out and flip through some other pages in the book, those of other students in her class. She read things like: *Parents separated. Eats at grandmother's house every day. Cumulative shortcomings from primary school. Cognitive problems. Attention Deficit? Hyperactive. Good personality, but difficulty conceptualizing. Need for social intervention. Bulimic. Attention seeking, possibly doesn't receive enough affection at home. Well-integrated. Competitive and responsible.* She slammed the book closed when she heard the guidance counselor's footsteps; the woman entered with the same smile as always—her neat teeth bound by very fine braces—and returned to her seat. Soon doesn't remember what they talked about. She kept thinking about what she'd read. She was terrified to think that the teachers shared those kinds of notes, that they talked about them, the students, exchanging their files like baseball cards. Old Man nods. Those files, he says, are like the ones they used at the hospital! The guardians of morality make their mental diagnoses by dissecting families, they never get past that! And it's always about mothers, one way or another, whether they're present or not, loved or not, whether they're young or old, abusive or controlling: even if they're dead, they're discussed! It bothered him when people talked about his mother. He got violently upset every time it happened, even when it only seemed like it might be happening—because they also talked about her behind his back, in whispers. There were a lot of files at the hospital, a lot of records, two or three rooms full of records in blue folders, hundreds, thousands of blue folders stuffed with records. He would have summed up his file in a single sentence: *This man needs to walk.* To walk alone, without anyone bothering him!, and that would have been enough. How simple! If you think about it, each one of the patients' files, or the students', could be summed up in a single sentence. What a bunch of wasted words!

Why were you there, Old Man?, Soon finally dares to ask. She doesn't think he's opposed to telling her; rather, he thinks of it as common knowledge, as if there were no need to explain or he'd just forgotten to do it. But Soon needs him to explain, even though he looks at her without understand-ing—there *where*?, he asks—and she has to specify: at the hospital, why were you a patient in that hospital? Old Man is sitting on the towel, back in his light-colored suit, fresh from the cleaners, with the handkerchief neatly folded and peeking out of his jacket pocket. The weather is harsh that morning, a cold wind shakes the Siberian elm's branches and the leaves fall around them—day by day, leaf by leaf, the tree is peeling itself onto them. Old Man is thinking, and she's afraid that now he's going to hedge, that it wasn't really a matter of forgetting, but of intentionally keeping a secret. But finally he speaks and says that it was all the fault of the mind police, he wasn't to blame, he didn't do anything to deserve being locked up. He was happy doing his work—back then he was working at the bird sanctuary, does Soon remember the sanctuary? But the mind police can't forgive happiness in people like him, people who don't have a mother and a father like everyone else, but a mother and a father-grandfather in one! Those people, monsters like him, he goes on—ever more upset, more rushed—aren't allowed to be happy!, and when they, the mind police, saw how well he was doing his work at the sanctuary, that he was efficient and professional, that he was punctual and showed good judgement, when they saw that all their theories about idiots and simpletons and cretins were falling apart and losing their validity, they got together and agreed to lock him up! They invented an excuse to do it, and *voilà*!

Old Man's eyes are burning now, his hair on end and his glasses crooked. As he's been speaking, he hung the binoculars around his neck, took them off, adjusted them, and put them around his neck again, his movements abrupt and nervous. Astonished, Soon stammers: your . . . father was also your grandfather? Yes, yes, you heard right!, he replies, taking the binoculars off again and throwing them far away, beyond the shrubs. Why do you have the same look as everyone else?, he asks and jumps up, stomping on the grass. A gust of cold wind blows between them, and Soon is flooded more by curiosity than fear.

Only after a silence, only after he's apologized, picked up the binoculars and made sure they weren't damaged, only when he starts to seem more composed—his breathing calmer, his gaze inoffensive—does she ask him to explain. Old Man, really, I don't understand, she whispers.

Well, at first he didn't understand either! It took him a long time to understand—he probably wasn't soon-to-be fourteen, but over fourteen, much older than fourteen! It's not strange for your father to also be your grandfather if no one has ever told you it's strange, right? For him, it was the most normal thing in the world! But when he did find out, he understood the evasive looks, the whispers, the house with no visitors, his mother, so silent, his father with his wrinkles and cane. It's a mistake that Old Man carries with him, like a steer marked with a brand, and that's why they locked him up, nothing more than that!

Since Old Man told her that he has a father-grandfather, Soon has been turning the idea over and over, constantly; she feels simultaneously attracted and repelled by it. She always heard that children born within the same family—the children of siblings, for example—are often defective, and so she's uncomfortable bringing it up, because it shows an unhealthy and almost insulting curiosity, and because her ideas and prejudices, after all, arise from the same place as those of the people he called *mind police*: his enemies. Still, she's intrigued. How could something like that happen? Does he see it as normal? And where is his family now? Did they abandon him? There are so many gaps in Old Man's life story, so many things she doesn't know, even though he talks and talks and talks . . . Like now, for example, when the imminent arrival of the cold has inspired him to describe bird migrations to Africa, and he explains that in recent years many species—the white stork!, the booted eagle!—have changed their routes because of climate change. It's hard to interrupt Old Man when he's expounding on all he knows, very difficult to throw in, out of nowhere, the wedge of personal and private matters. But Soon is alert and waiting for her chance, and she finds it later, when he recites

Nina Simone's "Blackbird" for her: *Why you wanna fly, Black-bird? / You ain't ever gonna fly*, and then translates the lyrics to Spanish. Apparently, the song was about the oppression black people suffered in those days, but maybe it's also about him—or even about both of them, who knows.

Old Man patiently teaches her the lyrics, and this, Nina Simone's "Blackbird," is what gives her the excuse to ask about his parents, specifically the lines *No place big enough for holding / All the tears you're gonna cry / Cause your mama's name was "Lonely," / And your daddy's name was "Pain."* *Soledad y Pena?*, says Soon, after Old Man translates the lyrics. Those are some names! It's true that Soledad is a name in Spanish—she has an Aunt Soledad—and Pena could well be a last name, but it's clear the song isn't referring to real names, but symbolic ones. But it's not symbolism she needs just then: she wants things to be exact, exact details, exact names, and that's why she plays dumb and asks—she finally goes for it and asks—what his parents' names are, if they're alive, or what their names were, if they are dead.

Old Man takes off his glasses and cleans them slowly with a tissue, which he unfolds and then carefully refolds and puts away. His father is dead, he says, he was old, much older than his mother, Soon already knows that! His name was Adrian and his mother, he says, Adriana: you can see his desire to possess was there from the start! There's a bitterness that creeps into his words—maybe for the first time—a kind of bitterness that's different from the fury he exudes when he talks about the clinic or climate change. But, is your mother still alive?, she ventures to ask. Yes, of course, his mother is still young, the thing is that he barely sees her, he's never really seen her very much, their relationship has always been distant, she could never overcome the aversion she felt for him. No one ever reproached her for it, they all considered her a little weird! He laughs when he says it: she was weird, I was crazy. That's how everyone knew them. But she isn't weird and he's not crazy. He just has his cerebral connections put together in a different way; certain connections, not all of them!, which means that there are some things he doesn't do very well—can't do very well—but when it comes to others, he's an ace, he has no competition!

His mother?, he repeats, lost in thought. She lives in a home, not all that different from his clinic—they share the same controlling spirit!—but at least they treat her well because she never gives them problems. When he goes to visit her, they hold hands and look each other in the eye, silently, very directly. In the past, his mother could never look at him like that, she always averted her eyes toward something else. Now, though, she stares at him anxiously, as though trying to recover all the time they lost. She seems to be searching for something with that look, some kind of answer! But it's not easy, you know?, says Old Man: it's not easy to meet such a direct gaze—so inquisitive! Try it, he challenges her, and he looks at Soon very seriously, his eyes open wide behind his newly cleaned glasses that have a little piece of tissue stuck to one arm, so solemn and so ridiculous, now holding back a smile to keep the game going, so willing to forget the drama, to change the subject, to lighten the situation, that finally they both burst out laughing.

The clinic was like her school, but on a larger scale. Just imagine, Old Man tells her, if you had to spend all day in there, within those walls!, with normal teachers, normal students, and normal classes. After a few days no one would be normal anymore, they'd all go crazy, don't you think? You only have to look at the desperation of birds in cages. Some of them bang against the bars, break their beaks trying to escape. Though those are the minority: most of them end up accepting their prisons and fall into a kind of perpetual listlessness. Domestic birds turn stupid and they sing, sure, but they sing half-heartedly—like automatons! In the clinic, instead of singing, the patients played Parcheesi or cards or they watched TV—documentaries, sedate movies, ones that wouldn't upset them. They were treated like children or elderly people, when many of them—many of us, he says—were young or middle-aged men and women. Soon would like to ask for more details about life in the mental hospital—she no longer has any doubt that it was a mental hospital—but the only thing she manages to ask is how long he was in there. Old Man shrugs his shoulders; he can't calculate it clearly. Time is different in there, he says. Longer?, asks Soon. No, not longer: different!, it's measured in another way!

The early days were the worst. They locked him in his room when he got nervous, which made him even more nervous. They forced him to take medicines even though he hadn't given his consent. I do not consent!, he'd protested, but as soon as he opened his mouth to object they stuffed a pill in it, and sometimes several people held him down and injected him with tranquilizers. They did that kind of thing to everyone to keep them good and calm, and they still had to be grateful there was no more electroshock! These days they call it electro-convulsive therapy! But they fry your brain the same!

Soon's compassion as she listens gives way to fascination: Old Man's life is ever more enigmatic and intriguing. Old Man has a father-grandfather and he was in an insane asylum—now she's using that phrase: *insane asylum*—he has a strange, dark past, he's been repudiated through a conspiracy of the mind police who locked him up by force. It's possible that later that day, when she pretends to do her homework sitting serenely at her desk with her bedroom door closed, she will write about all of this, embellishing it here and there with a fitting tone: *Little by little he reveals his secrets; he whispers them quietly into my ear; I tremble as I listen; his voice is hoarse and slow, like the bad guys in scary movies, but he isn't bad, I don't think he's bad, though maybe he's done evil things.*

So your father was a monster, then. A monster? No, why? No more monstrous than the people who tortured Old Man at the clinic! His father loved them. Both of them, his mother and him. Old Man doesn't have bad memories of him, not at all! He does remember him, it's true, as awkward, curt, a man of few words. Big. Very big! Almost two meters tall, he says, and luckily Old Man didn't inherit that height, because being so tall only gives you back problems. Shy. He was also shy! His teeth were in very bad shape because he was ashamed to open his mouth in front of a dentist. He never, ever went to the doctor. He barely had any friends. Because he was shy, not evil!, insists Old Man. He went to work at the factory—he was a pipe fitter—came home, helped his daughter with the housework—like that, day after day, all his life! On weekends they went to church together: he was a very devout man, but he never took communion. Sometimes he drank a lot, he drank until he passed out, but that didn't happen every day, and he never got violent. He loved her a lot, his daughter, his Adriana. So much that he wouldn't let her go out; he was afraid something would happen to her. He shooed away any man who approached her, and also, later on, any woman! Back then girls didn't go out as much as they do now. It was the normal way of things for his mother to spend all her time inside. No one thought it was odd, although it was precisely her being shut away that must have caused what happened to happen. Old Man sincerely believes that his father didn't do it with evil intentions. He must have gotten things confused! The neighbors presumed that his mother had slipped up and gotten pregnant, by who knew whom. That's what they thought, or wanted to think, in spite of the fact that he, Old Man, had no problem calling his father *dad*. He called him *dad* and not *grandpa,* in public places, in the plaza, in the small corner store where they bought provisions. As a child he spent more time with his father-grandfather than with his mother, who always avoided him, tending hurriedly to his needs without ever speaking or playing. Later, when he grew up, it took him a long time to understand—he was at least sixteen years old when he fit the puzzle together! He forced himself to hate his father-grandfather, unsuccessfully. When he found out the truth, from exactly that day onward, his life twisted up and turned unhappy. That's why he started to look for consolation in birds. Only when he was observing or reading about birds did he feel secure. He discovered, for example, that incest is normal among certain species. There are tons of birds that copulate happily with each other and never stop to think whether it's correct or not. Who has the right to tell them it's wrong, that they should stop it immediately? Certainly not him! Luckily, birds have saved him from resentment, among other things.

Soon waits for him, biting her nails, a knot in her belly, shivering. It's no longer pleasant at the hideout in the morning, especially on sunless days, when the damp grass never dries and the dew soaks through her clothes and seeps into her skin, a dirty feeling all day long, reminding her of her deception. The deception she is living within, thinks Soon, that deception—that sham—that has everything to do with the certified letter she now has in her pocket. Old Man comes through the bushes and opens his arms with a smile. What happened to you yesterday? Why didn't you come?, he asks. I had a fever, Old Man, she tells him, and my throat hurt, but that's not important, it was actually lucky, if you think about it, because just by chance she was there alone when the mailman came, so she was the one who received the letter and signed for it. The mailman is lazy and apathetic and he turns a blind eye at delivering a letter to a minor like

Soon: another stroke of luck. The fact is, the letter is in her hands.

She gives it to him straightaway and Old Man reads it slowly, moving his lips in silence, still standing, visible to any workers who might pass nearby—this one time, it doesn't matter. A copy of the file transfer, he says, that's what they're asking for, right? She nods, swallows. A paper that should have been handed in when the old registration was cancelled, and that is essential. There's a deadline, she says, did he read the letter to the end? Fifteen business days, she says—she doesn't fully know what *business* means in this context, but she does know that *fifteen days* sounds soon, very soon. What are we going to do?, asks Old Man, and she is comforted that he speaks in plural, because it means the problem is now both of theirs, and he's not going to abandon her. What are we going to do?, he repeats, but his question isn't a lament; rather, he's really trying to come up with an answer, to get out of the problem, to solve it. What if we fake the document?, suggests Soon. All they'd have to do is find an example online and copy it, stamp it—even with a stamp from something else, any stamp will do. Héctor, the boy who skipped school so much, faked dozens of doctor's notes that slipped through the cracks for years before he was found out. The point is to buy some time, says Soon, but a gust of cold air shakes the tree and a handful of leaves falls onto them, reminding them that buying time doesn't matter, because the time will come all the same, and soon it will be winter.

We could do nothing!, says Old Man. He knows from experience that sometimes deadlines are not met, and nothing happens. This—he says, shaking the letter in his hand—this, he repeats, is nothing but a bureaucratic formality, a letter that someone printed and sent because it was time to do it!, but one they won't follow up on closely, you'll see. Someone, a different person, will have to remember that there was a deadline and that the deadline has passed; someone will have to realize that, in effect, no one has responded to the document request; someone will have to consult the next measures that must be set in motion, and then set them in motion! If along the way someone—another someone—decided to contact her parents by phone, they would find out it's a wrong number, which could bring up further doubts, but . . . that's also called buying time! Soon listens to Old Man's reasoning, and his confidence as he analyzes future possibilities is comforting. Look, he says, kneeling down beside her, putting his hand on her arm—putting his hand on her *arm*, Soon recognizes—we still have a lot of time. They might send a second and a third request before they take any more drastic measures. That's how it often is, he explains, bureaucracy has its deadlines, they're unavoidable, they approach slowly, step by step—but slowly!

The mind police also had their way with Nina Simone. To explain away her rage and demean the racial protests of her songs, they diagnosed her with mental illnesses, they medicated her and took her out of action! Her androgyny, they said, must be related to bipolarity. Her rage, to psychotic breaks. But what about all the people who admired her?

Were they crazy too? He cackles, caught up in his tirade. Do you know who Nick Cave is?, he asks then. Very slowly Soon repeats: Nick Cave . . . no. Who is he? One of the many musicians who adored her. They shared a stage at the end of the nineties, and by then they'd really done a number on Nina! Before the concert, someone came in and asked her if she wanted anything. Nina was lying down with her eyes closed, and she raised her head, opened her eyes, and you know what she asked for? The scene reminds Soon of those movies where prisoners condemned to die are asked what they want for their last meal. What did she ask for, Old Man?, she inquires. And he replies, oh, this is great, Nina said: I'd like some champagne, some cocaine, and some sausages. Champagne, cocaine, and sausages!, he repeats. It's a brilliant answer! Tremendous! Soon doesn't understand why it's so tremendous. She suspects that it's only because Nina said it, reason enough for Old Man. And did they give it to her?, she asks reservedly, startled at Old Man's casual yet fascinated manner when he mentions cocaine. Yes, of course they did, you don't refuse a diva anything! Before she started to sing, Nina took her gum out of her mouth and left it stuck to the side of the piano; supposedly, Nick Cave's violinist, Warren Ellis, put it in a napkin and he still has it, like a relic. Old Man has written to Nick Cave's label offering to buy that gum! He's offered thousands of dollars—dollars he doesn't have, of course, although who knows, the point is to take the first step—but he never got a reply! And why does he want a piece of chewed-up gum? That's lame, Old Man, murmurs Soon with a trace of disdain.

(When Old Man talks about his diva so devotedly, she confronts a previously unknown blend of feelings, one that includes, no doubt about it, jealously.)

All the girls in my class have boyfriends, she blurts out suddenly, on impulse, staring at the ground and digging her sneakers into the dirt. Old Man looks at her without understanding what that assertion means to her, whether she thinks it's a good thing or not. Oh, no, I don't care, she replies when he asks her, it's just that they *all* have boyfriends, like it's in fashion; last year none of them did—or maybe just one or two, the most developed ones—and now they all do, they couple up as soon as they can, even if they don't like the boy they happen to get, just because, or because not having a boyfriend means you're a loser. What about you? Do you have a boyfriend? She shakes her head hard. No, of course not, gross. She will never have a boyfriend, never ever. Boys are disgusting. Always playing pranks, always competing with each other. So rough and stupid. And what do the girls do with their boyfriends? Soon answers reluctantly, seeming to forget she was the one who started this conversation: they go to the movies or the mall, they hide in the parks to make out, on weekends they meet up at the underage club, the one that closes at eleven at night, an awful place: she went one time and never wants to go back.

Old Man sits in silence with a worried expression. But Soon, he finally cries, there's nothing wrong with falling in love! It'll happen to you one day and you'll understand! He

82

has fallen in love many times and it's wonderful! As if the whole world were spread with butter and everything was more flavorful and better! She raises an eyebrow in disdain: that's some comparison, she thinks. Plus, she's already been in love, she tells him haughtily, and she knows what it's like: it's horrible, gross, she'll never do it again. This all happened a while ago, before her brother left, when she was twelve years old. Back then, her brother had a friend who went everywhere with him. That guy, the friend, is who she fell in love with. She had never felt anything like that for anyone. She spent the whole day thinking about him, dreaming about him. She'd be alone in her room, and suddenly his name would come out of her mouth, involuntarily, and she would delight in that name, in repeating his name and writing it a thousand times, everywhere: on the wall, in her notebooks, on the back of her hand, and on the fogged-up mirror. Her heart leapt every time she heard him come into the house with her brother. Though her trembling legs betrayed her, she'd go out to see him, feigning indifference, trying to seem interesting—a book under her arm, half-closed eyes, walking barefoot with her anklet tinkling. Hi, she'd say, and all the heat in the world would rise into her cheeks. Hi, he'd reply, and that one syllable—the memory of it—could keep Soon entertained for days. One afternoon, her brother wasn't home when his friend came looking for him. Her mother let him in to wait, saying he wouldn't be long. Soon got the idea to walk over to him and pretend to look for something in the chest of drawers he was sitting next to. Her mother was far away when he asked her what grade she was in—as if he didn't know—clearly wanting to start a conversation. They talked for a while, about this and that. She let her guard down, batted her lashes to beguile him. She'd prepared herself for the occasion: sitting beside him, legs crossed, she told him everything she'd found out about the rock group she knew he liked. He smiled, gave her an unexpected kiss on the lips. Soon pulled back in surprise, but then she leaned toward him to repeat it. This time, the boy pulled away. Clever girl, he said, and then: Do you know that you're going to be very pretty someday? You're *going to be*, in the future, Soon emphasizes: you see? He was letting her know that she wasn't pretty then, that she wasn't good enough for him yet. When her brother arrived, Soon scuttled away in shame. But she could hear them as they were leaving. The friend told him: I think your little sister has a crush on me. And then he said: poor thing. *Poor thing.* Her brother laughed: don't even think about coming near my sister, he threatened, but he clearly said it as a joke, not to defend her but just the opposite, to attack her, portraying her to his friend as a little girl, a poor idiot girl, the little sister. Of course she's not going to fall in love ever again, repeats Soon. She'll never have a boyfriend, never get married, never have children, never do any of those things everyone expects a girl to do just so they can laugh at you in the end. Everyone laughs at sisters, at wives, and at mothers, or they insult you by invoking them. But Soon will not be any of those things. She's not even anyone's sister anymore, because her brother left the country and now it's as if she didn't have a brother, as if she'd never met him.

One day she starts to cry suddenly, unexpectedly, and Old Man pulls her into his lap. The physical intimacy created in that moment—sudden, spontaneous—is new for them, and makes them both uncomfortable. Still, they stay in the same position for several minutes, breathing in the same rhythm, his hands patting her hair—his first caresses—while she lets her arms rest on his legs, her head on his belly. Old Man doesn't ask why she's crying. A question like that is superfluous: one should be able to intuit the answer. Nor does Soon go to the trouble of giving explanations. She knows he's not expecting them. It's calm, there's nothing but that calm, broken only by the song of a blue tit—that's the only thing Old Man says: hear that?, a blue tit—and the cold air, the approaching winter, the wind a signal of menace.

I'm not afraid of dying, she says proudly. She believes in reincarnation. She's read some books that prove it through scientific evidence. She would like to be reincarnated as a cat, but not just any cat, but a wild one, a street cat. Street cats are free, she says, and they're beautiful, and they don't give explanations to anyone about anything, and they spend the whole day sleeping and grooming themselves, and at night they go out looking for trouble. Old Man crosses his arms. What if he comes back as a bird? If, for example, he lived in the little body of a sparrow? She would hunt him, she'd torture him and stun him with a swipe of her cat claw, and then with the other she'd grab him by the neck and devour him in one bite! No, no, Soon sets him straight, she would recognize him right away, it doesn't matter what body one reincarnates into because there are always vestiges of the soul that remain—that's the correct term, according to what she's read, *vestiges of the soul.* Those vestiges are revived at the right stimuli, and memories are unlocked, she affirms with certainty. In that case, says Old Man, we should have memories of our past souls, if in the past we were something different from what we are now. Soon is serious as she reflects. It's true, she concludes, that must be it, that's why the two of them feel close, they've recognized each other because in previous lives they must've also been very close. Maybe they were flamingos crossing the Strait of Gibraltar together, or they rowed beside Cervantes in a galley; maybe they harvested cotton side by side in Alabama, or maybe they were sibling cats in Ancient China or cows in India or a human mother and son in Siberia. She looks at Old Man sideways, dives in: could it be that they were even boyfriend and girlfriend, in other bodies and in another place, but still, boyfriend and girlfriend? Right away she bites her lips, embarrassed by her own audacity.

(The end is coming, it's arriving with the cold that has settled in definitively, even in that city where it's hardly ever cold, and with the workers who maybe—just maybe—are starting to get suspicious. Soon wears her down coat and doesn't intend to take it off all day long, and brings a fleece sweatshirt that she sits on to wait for her friend. Haste, or need, is coming to a boil inside her, the need to force a denouement in keeping with her rebellion, so blind and unproductive. Or maybe she simply confuses things, mixes up what is expected, what is feared, and what is presupposed, so that it fits with what is, which has no name. She collects ambiguous moments, reads into them with her sick and neurotic gaze. Men cannot be friends with girls, she's always been told that, and even more: it's *impossible* for an *old man* to make friends with a *young girl*. An old man deceives, has hidden intentions—dirty intentions. That is the natural thing, not the opposite, and what they say generally about old men is also applicable to Old Man, to the actual Old Man, *her* Old Man, thus sweeping away all his particularities and exceptions. To top it all off Old Man is very strange, he doesn't do anything, doesn't work, he wears binoculars everywhere he goes, he spends all his time reading about birds and pouring over the lyrics of Nina Simone songs. Old Man had a father-grandfather and a mother who wouldn't look at him; they locked him in a clinic where they had to tie him down and medicate him so he wouldn't attack anyone; Old Man only has two suits, one for summer and another for winter, and when he takes them to the cleaners he wears clothes he got from a friend who killed himself. She intuits that Old Man is poor, but she loves to imagine him as a rich old man; she intuits that he is harmless, but if she wants to get somewhere with this, she has to imagine him as dangerous. She can't end up without a story to tell. She needs a story to tell.

She writes in her diary: sometimes a line, but other times several pages, paragraphs and paragraphs about her invented life, a life where no one calls her *marshmallow*, where Marga isn't a classmate who bullies her, where her brother isn't the brother who left, where her brother's friend never referred to her as *poor thing*, and Old Man is not the Old Man who has just come through the shrubbery and looked up through his binoculars, wrinkling his eyes, trying to identify exactly what kind of parakeet it is that has landed on the Siberian elm's highest branch.)

Old Man, the other day I talked to a neighbor about you. He has brought, to show her, what he calls *a treasure*: a French ornithological treatise from the early twentieth century, its pages eaten away—it's like lace, he says, caressing the edges—and with beautiful full-color illustrations of *perroquets* and *cygnes*. A fortune, he'd told her when he arrived—it cost him a fortune!—but even so he had to buy it, he'd found it at a used bookstore buried under a bunch of worthless books—a shame, a shame, it needed to be rescued! Are you listening to me?, insists Soon, arms crossed, chin down. Old Man looks up, thinks about the words she has said. Why?, he asks. What do you mean, why? A different question would have been more logical, for example *about what?*, what was it that she'd said about him, but *why*? You told me you didn't have any friends, says Old Man, still distracted, stealthily turning the pages of his treatise. She's not a friend, replies Soon, I told you, she's a neighbor. A neighbor my age, she specifies. And why did you talk to her about me?, he repeats, with real disinterest. Gnawing at her fingernails, Soon doesn't know how to go on. She wanted to know what her neighbor thought. Old Man puts down the treatise, sets it gently aside, and looks at her—finally—with attention. What she thinks *about what*? Soon tears up blades of grass and shreds them between her fingers as she speaks. What she thinks of us being friends, of you coming here every day to see me, of you helping me skip school and all that. I help you skip school? No, it's not exactly help, stammers Soon, it's more that you don't judge me and you help me figure out what to do, like not responding to the request for documentation, for example. And what does she think about me, this neighbor of yours?, asks Old Man. She advised me to ask you directly. Ask me what? If you would be here with any other girl, or if it's only me. I don't understand, he says. If what you need is someone to talk to, about your birds and about Nina Simone and those things of yours, some company that any other person could also give you—a boy, a girl, a man, or a woman—or if it's me in particular, because of something I have and you like. Of course it's you, I don't stop to talk to the park workers or the woman who sells me my buns every day, I come here for you! But why?, Soon wants to know, and now she's the one who is asking *why*. Is there something about her that he likes? Something that makes him come back day after day? Something she has now or that he hopes to get from her someday? She feels in a hurry to get somewhere, to reach some conclusion, and Old Man is not making it easy. Men like young girls, isn't that right? She looks down, ashamed. Is that what's happening between them? No, no, no . . . Old Man screws up his face. No, he repeats, he swears to her, it's not that, she shouldn't be afraid!

Who has made her think like that? Did her neighbor put those thoughts in her head? Hadn't they agreed they'd met in another life and that's why they've recognized each other?

Now she is quiet, trying to figure out where the problem is. So Old Man doesn't like her? Is it because she is ugly, because she's fat, because of the zits on her arms, because she's never experienced anything worth talking about, because she doesn't have the hoarse and seductive voice that other girls have? Because of her marshmallow body? A lot of girls get harassed by men. She's heard the stories. It happens all the time. They get harassed online, for example. And in person, too. By tutors who give piano or English lessons. The afternoon tennis instructors, or swim coaches. Neighbors. Their friends' fathers. So what's wrong with her? Is she not attractive to anyone? Not even to Old Man? He has returned now to his treatise—his treasure—and he's showing her the illustrations as if that conversation had never happened. She bites her lip, tries to stop her chin from trembling.

These are absolutely not good days. Soon's stomach is churning with anxiety. The threat is lurking just around the corner—or in her case, through the hedges—and it gets closer and closer every day. This time things are really a mess. She tells Old Man the story in a labored voice. She was having lunch with her parents, she says, when someone rang the doorbell—a policeman. All three of them got really scared, so it wasn't suspicious—or not too much—when Soon burst out crying as soon as she saw him. The cop soothed them, I'm only here to deliver a document, he told them, it's just a formality, but it has to be done like this, by official delivery, a document from the school inspectorate, or social services, Soon didn't understand that part very well. Did you see it?, asks Old Man. No, just the outside, but she heard her parents talking about it, the paper didn't say what it was about, or even ask for any documentation. It was a mandatory appointment—a summons, both of her parents called it—a date, a time, and a place, and it's within a few days. Okay, says Old Man, if it's in a few days, they could very well forget!

Soon shudders. How could they forget? They're really worried! Of course, they asked if there was something she hadn't told them. Things like: Has anyone given you trouble? Have they hurt you? Threatened you? Have they asked you for money? Soon said no to everything. None of their questions came at all close to the truth. Maybe if her parents had asked the right question she wouldn't have been able to deny it, but for them it's impossible to imagine what she's really been doing for the past two months, soon to be three. Her mother suggested calling the teacher to try to find out what the problem was, and then Soon did break down, she threw herself to the floor, got on her knees and begged her not to do it. The teacher never stopped ridiculing her in front of the other kids, she lied. Better to keep her out of it, please, please. Her mother was taken aback. All right, she said. She promised not to call and to wait for the appointment, though Soon doesn't know if she'll keep her promise or if she only made it to calm her daughter down. She fears the latter.

Old Man spreads out the towel, takes out a couple bags of chips and offers her one. Gruyere, he tells her—it's a new flavor! Soon clutches her head in her hands. Old Man doesn't understand anything, she thinks, he doesn't realize that it's a matter of days, or hours, before they find her out, before another cop comes to her house and arrests her. The game is going to end, and Soon is afraid, and she's in a hurry. She doesn't know what's going to happen, or how it's going to happen, and she doesn't know the steps she must take to bring it about.

But something has to happen, and it has to be now.

It's easier to imagine confessing it later, telling a girlfriend, for example—even Marga—or a guy friend—even better, a guy friend—flaunting a tormented and decadent air, the aura of a bad girl, an abused girl, a girl who had a brush with danger and lived to tell about it. Old Man doesn't notice the change in her, her sudden determination, which complicates things because she'll have to start from scratch, without any help from him. Old Man, she says, but she doesn't know how to go on. Old Man, she repeats, and she looks at him, begging for his cooperation, but he doesn't understand. What's wrong, Soon? You don't want to try them?, he says, offering her the chips again. No, she says, and then, like a spark—and where does that intuition, that wisdom, come from?—I don't feel good, it hurts here, in my leg. Your leg? Why does your leg hurt? Did you hit it, did you fall? Yes, I fell, and she moans, but her moan is singsong, unconvincing. Old Man gets up, comes closer, let me see, he says, just what she wanted to hear. Soon stands up too, but—unexpectedly—she's overcome with shame, an intense modesty at the prospect of showing herself—of showing him even just a bit of her flesh—and she points over her tracksuit pants: here, it hurts here. But did you cut yourself, are you bleeding, is it a bruise? What is it, Soon? In an impulse, she pulls down her pants.

(And it's no coincidence that the song of a starling scratches the silence created between the two of them. She recognizes it: a starling, she thinks. She's well-trained now.)

Soon is in her underwear with her sweatpants around her knees. Old Man, more bewildered by her abruptness than by the sight of her naked thighs, takes a step back. I don't see anything, he says, and then she pulls down her underpants. Do you see something now?, she screams.

Old Man lurches backward, covers his face in horror, fingers outstretched, his fat fingers, ugly and freckled. What are you doing, what did I do to you?, he asks, as if she were submitting him to punishment. She is stock-still. She's really turned to stone, her arms and legs stiff; all the heat rises to her face and the rest of her body freezes, turns to ice. Cover yourself, Soon, whispers Old Man, still hiding his face behind his fingers, and it takes her a while to do it because her muscles won't obey her as they should. She can tell he's scared, but she's not sure why. Is it because the park workers could catch him right now, in this predicament? Or is it because she horrifies him, because she disgusts him? She bursts out crying, every bit as disconcerted as he is. Old Man comes closer as if he wanted to console her, but then he backs away again, while his fingers lower little by little down his face, leaving his widened eyes in view, changed eyes that look at her in a way they never had before. Soon has pulled up her pants now, and she wipes her tears with a forearm, sobbing. Her desperation is also new; never, ever, has she felt this anguish. She's the one who flings herself at him, the one who hugs him trembling, pressing herself against Old Man's rigid body. Don't you like me?, she asks. Don't you like me? Old Man is silent and she puts her hand on his pants, looks for him. She doesn't know what comes next, she can't get past the zipper. Old Man doesn't move, he only pants softly, with a high-pitched sound somewhere between a moan and a sob, and his breathing grows deeper and more animal. Soon looks for him while he wants to flee, his body stiff—both of their bodies—like a cadaver's. She is still crying and he pants more softly, on the verge of tears. They move apart. Their eyes meet for a second, less than a second, and they can't stand it. Soon looks down, hunches over as if she'd been hit. Old Man grabs his backpack from the ground, yells something unintelligible, and takes off running. He crosses through the hedges so violently that the branches keep shaking for a while, even when she can no longer hear the sound of his footsteps running away.

The emptiness that follows is immense, as immense as the pain, the shame, the desperation she feels as she looks up at the sky, immense as the cold, the dampness that permeates her clothes and creeps into her skin, immense as the silence—above all, the silence. Where is Old Man? Has she really lost him forever? How is it possible that everything remains the same except for him, who isn't here? If only she had a way to find him, if she at least had his phone number— but, after all, what could she say to him? She would choke on the words. What she wants is to see him, it would be enough just to see him. She could look for him in the streets where he told her he lived; she doesn't know which block exactly but she could investigate the mailboxes. She could even ask about him—*an old man with glasses and a backpack and binoculars always wears a light suit and a giant coat talks weird likes birds.* However, the very thought of doing this shows how absurd, how inadequate it all is. She decides to wait. She closes her eyes and invokes him. Come back, Old Man, don't be mad at me, don't reject me, I couldn't live with it, they're going to catch me soon and I won't be able to come back ever again.

She's told it differently in her diary. She can't tell the truth, so shameful. This time she doesn't choose her words carefully, nor does she endeavor to improve her handwriting as she normally does. She writes fast, in a hurry, feeling relieved as she fills the page but very bad when she finishes and rereads what she's written. The words are contradictory, they're full of lies like sharp edges, they wound so.

Old Man returns on the fourth day like this: weepy, trembling, begging. Never, absolutely never, can she repeat what she did the other day. Soon, swear you won't do it ever again. And she swears, raises her right hand, closes her eyes, she promises, she promises.

Old Man, you have to forgive me, she says, and he—who doesn't shout today, today he only whispers—tells her that in a different park he found a lost Agapornis, very sad, very disoriented, and he bought some seeds that, with a lot of patience, he got it to eat. She understands that this is his way of forgiving her: talking about his birds, as if nothing bad had happened.

She would like to do the same, to go on just like that, but in her situation going on means failing, her position isn't the same as Old Man's. There's very little time left before the meeting with the educational inspectorate—or social services, Soon still doesn't know—just a few days, she can count them on one hand, and she's afraid that even before the meeting, at any moment, the police will show up at her house again and shame her parents definitively. This is what she most fears: shaming her parents. Nothing she has done was done against them. She doesn't care about disappointing them—she's already disappointed them many times—but she doesn't want to hurt them. She imagines the two cops looking at each other, confounded, murmuring: how is it possible that this girl has skipped school almost three months and they, her parents, have been so oblivious?

Old Man has a wound on his hand, a deep cut that looks infected. He's put a bandage on it that doesn't cover as much as it should; the skin, swollen and bruised, bares itself brazenly around it. The bandage is dirty and ragged. But Soon is not going to ask him what happened. And not just out of deference. Maybe she doesn't want to know. Maybe it's better to act like him, to talk about nothing but birds.

We could go live together, she says without thinking. Where?, he asks. She likes that he doesn't question the statement itself—about living together—but rather the practical aspects: where, how, when. She doesn't know where, but far away—or maybe not that far, she says, not so far that she couldn't visit her parents every once in a while. Old Man sits thinking: they could live on a lake, or a pond, so they could observe the cycles of birds, the courting, the nesting, the migrations. Would she like that? Soon gets excited, nods. Maybe it would be easier if they got married, she says, because if they don't get married people could come looking for her and take her away from there—from the lake or wherever—by force. They might think Old Man has kidnapped her or seduced her by pouring a potion into her drink, like in fairy tales. If they get married, though, it won't be so easy to separate them, there'll be papers joining them, it'll take lawyers or judges or whatever to invalidate those papers, and that will take a long time, very long, and meanwhile Soon will have birthdays and she'll come of age.

He knows of a pond close to some pine forests, a place where the sunsets seem like another world. They could build a wooden cabin in the style of the old fishermen's shacks. They'd buy a used jeep so Soon could go to the city once she gets her driver's license. Maybe by then she'll have a friend, and they can see movies or go shopping together. He, Old Man, isn't crazy about the movies, and much less about shopping!, but he understands that Soon could have other needs.

We need to plan this more slowly, he says, there's no rush, and Soon is invaded, suddenly, by the suspicion that he's giving her the runaround. How can there be no rush? It's a matter of days, or hours, before they catch her! Old Man raises his wounded, badly bandaged hand. Easy, he says. I swear we'll do it. Later on, but we'll do it, he repeats, and he points at her: as long as what happened the other day never happens again. What happened the other day can never, ever happen again!

She nods, promises, even laughs.

Finally, a promise that's easy to keep.

Part Two

THE CAFÉ

YOU'VE GROWN, SOON. You're fourteen now. You're *more* than fourteen!

But he can't call her More. What an ugly name. She can still be Soon, if she wants! Soon to be fifteen. Soon to be sixteen! She'll always be something else soon. She has her whole life ahead of her.

Old Man has changed, too. His face is thinner, and two new wrinkles run down his cheeks from top to bottom, as though sliced by a razor. He is also paler. Have you been sick?, Soon asks, and he makes an ambiguous gesture with his head, maybe a negation, but only maybe. She thinks about the days he spent in a cell before they exonerated him. She heard that they didn't give him the medication he needed and that, despite his nervous fits, no doctor came to see him. She didn't even know that Old Man took medication, or that he could suffer fits. There were a lot of things she didn't know about him.

Soon is no longer a marshmallow. Or at least it's been a long time since anyone said she was. Marga switched schools and took most of the nicknames with her. In fact, when she left, the whole school put an end to that phase. But "marshmallow" is a concept that Soon still hasn't managed to shake off entirely. A concept that has to do with the way she pulls down her shirt to hide her body, or wears long sleeves in spite of the heat. With the hair hanging over her face and her baggy clothes.

Now, when she hears Old Man calling her Soon again, she's overcome by a deep happiness mixed with regret and nostalgia. I'm really sorry, Old Man, she says, I'm sorry for everything you went through because of me. Because of her? No, no, no. Old Man shakes his head hard. Why would it be Soon's fault?

(Of course, she doesn't dare tell him about the diary. About everything she wrote about him in her diary.)

It's ironic that in the end she was betrayed by her own big mouth. Not because of any missing documents in her supposed school transfer. Not because her teachers were checking up on her or because her classmates missed her. Not because the educational inspectorate informed her parents. Not because of the park workers. They, the workers, hadn't made the slightest attempt, either, to find out what was going on every day in the park, even though it would have been easy to notice her—notice them—or suspect the kind of dangers that might be nesting in the hedges. Soon wonders: if it hadn't been for her diary, would they have even found out about Old Man's existence? The secret of her truancy hung by a thread, it was only a matter of time—of hours—before she was found out, but he could have been saved from the fire. Every page she wrote in her notebook was a small, sure step toward his condemnation. The more she made up, the more reality slipped from her hands. As she altered Old Man, she destroyed him.

The hideout in the park . . . What has become of the hideout in the park? It took her a long time to go back, months and months—she'd been unequivocally forbidden from going. And when she did, it was afternoon and the light fell at a different angle, so different it didn't seem like the same place. That was exactly the feeling she had when she stopped and looked over the hedges: unfamiliarity. They'd planted new bushes, a double line of them that couldn't be crossed as easily as before. The tree shone golden under the sun. Looked at from afar, it was also another tree, more majestic and less welcoming. It's not easy to sum up these impressions in precise words. All she says is that she went back as soon as she could, though she knew she wasn't going to find him there. She admits she felt sad—though more than sadness, it was a shapeless unease that she doesn't try to name. Old Man rubs his eyes. It was a long time before he went back, too. He was terrified he'd be seen there! No one had forbidden him from going, of course; he could go wherever he wanted, as long as he complied with the restraining order! Although, how could he be sure to comply when he didn't know exactly where Soon was? It's an absurd order, Old Man doesn't know her address, or what school she goes to, or the route she walks every day. He could have found her sitting there again, like on the first day . . . and they would have arrested him immediately! Even so, he risked it, he couldn't help it. The park is right next to his house, how could he avoid it forever? The first days, when he dared to go back, he had to endure suspicious glances from the workers. Once, a cop even stopped him, asked for his documentation, wanted to know what he was doing there, and then let him go, just like that! Little by little his confidence grew. Until finally he peered in. The grass was overgrown, and there were a couple of blackbirds pecking at the ground in search of earthworms. They looked at him scornfully and went back to what they were doing. The hideout wasn't theirs anymore! It had other owners now!

Did it make you sad?, asks Soon. Old Man thinks about it before answering. No, not exactly, no . . . Blackbirds may be a plague, but they're still birds!

Soon has always wondered why the simplest things are often so hard to believe. When it was her turn to explain herself, she got stuck, she hedged, she felt like she was lying even when she told the whole truth. Everyone was against her, and she, somehow, found herself with no choice but to turn against everyone. Who was that man, how had she met him, why did she see him every day, what did he want from her? Suddenly, she had to put it all into words, everything that hadn't needed any words at all, or at least not the kind they were demanding. Who was that man?—that was something the girl couldn't say. All she could say was who he'd been for her, but that part of Old Man was hers alone, she couldn't share it with anyone even if she wanted to. Plus, what they really wanted to find out—full name, ID number, address, family history, medical record, criminal record, etc.—she didn't know, because she'd never really been curious to find out: that was the difference between them, between those who asked—insistent, tenacious, with violence hidden behind the soothing tone adults use to talk to children—and her, the one being questioned.

Her answers—unsatisfactory, improbable—only served to lend more credibility to her diary: it was easier to believe that everything had happened than to admit that, possibly, nothing had.

(Of course, there were contradictions when it came to the diary—those between what she said and what she wrote, and even contradictions between what she wrote on one page and the next—though at that point Soon still didn't know that they had read it, what an outrage.)

They told me you assaulted a woman, that you forced yourself on her. That precedent—that's what they called it: a *precedent*—was what raised the alarm. She had to put the puzzle together herself, and eventually she realized they were talking about the woman from the bird sanctuary, the keeper. That's why they locked him up in the mental hospital, not for any other reason. Now Soon wants to know the truth. She wants to hear how he defends himself.

Old Man shakes his head. I didn't assault anyone, he says, I never touched that woman, Soon. They've told you the story all wrong! At the most, you could call it harassment. Maybe the word *harass* is similar to *assault* and someone mixed them up out of confusion or pure spite, but they're very different! People tell the story wrong and it's repeated like that, all wrong, everyone spreading that horrible lie. He squeezes his temples with his hands. How can Soon doubt him? Does she really believe that story is possible?

She doesn't know how to answer. She's heard so many disconcerting things said about Old Man that she's unable to make up her mind. They were stories that incriminated him, turned him into someone completely different from who he is—or who she thought he was. The problem was that that deformed, perverted and adulterated vision of Old Man had its own internal logic, a logic that fit with what she had written in her diary. And so?

Harassment, assault, they're not the same thing, he protests, and I didn't even harass her! He liked to watch her from afar, it's true, he followed her along the paths sometimes, and once he managed to get inside her house and hide in the closet to watch her take a nap. That's all, that's all! No one had explained to him that you couldn't do that, it was inappropriate. If they'd explained, like the day when the police had informed him it was forbidden to talk to children, he would have followed the rules. But they never, ever gave him a chance. And they're not giving him one now, either!

Champagne, cocaine, and sausages. That was, apparently, what they'd consumed one sunny morning in the hideout. Old Man had spent his good money on the alcohol and drugs, which Soon, of course, didn't try—except for one sip of champagne, mmm, tasty. He applauded her behavior, didn't try to get such a young girl to enjoy forbidden delicacies, although if she wanted to, one day . . . They did both eat the sausages. They were smoked, stuffed with cheese, the kind that come in a jar cut up into little slices, gourmet snacks to stave off midday hunger. They ate them with sliced bread and gave all the leftovers to the pigeons. *What a strange lunch,* Soon wrote that day, omitting the chorizo sandwich, the Cheetos-stained fingers, and the little water bottle refilled at the fountain.

The waitress interrupts them again. It's the third time she's approached their table. The first time was to take their order. The second was to ask if they wanted anything else. No, they said. Now she's back again to insist. They must have been sitting there for two hours without consuming anything. But they don't have any more money. Soon, at least, has none.

Old Man searches his pockets discreetly—with his clumsy discretion—and asks for two glasses of water. Tap water, please! The waitress sighs, seems offended—the way she turns around, stalks over to the counter. She takes her time bringing them the water and she does it rudely, slamming the glasses down on the table without a word. The water is hot; when she takes a sip, Soon tastes soap. She and Old Man look at each other in silence. He doesn't even notice the contempt he receives. Maybe he's used to it. But Soon—who still hasn't hit fifteen and whose knowledge of the world is limited—is capable of seeing that in this cafe, the problem isn't her, it's him. In spite of her age, her inexperience, and her once-marshmallow body, she could fit in there—she *will* fit in there soon, in just a few years. She'll be like those other girls sitting at the table in back, talking and laughing—their laughter like chirping—ditzy, nervous, silly. But he, Old Man, no longer has time to adapt. The world would have to turn upside down for him not to stand out with his old-fashioned suit, his little glasses, his unkempt mustache, his arhythmical diction, and the damp, different gaze of the unbalanced.

Both of them are bothered by their environment, but for different reasons. Old Man says: we're used to being alone, this is very strange! But on top of that she feels a trace of embarrassment, not exactly because people are seeing her with him, with that eccentric Old Man, but because she is witness to the way he is treated, and she knows she can't do anything to defend him.

She would like him to tell her more details. What happened when he was arrested. Where exactly they took him. What they asked him. What they did to him. Soon's knowledge only comes from fragments, unconnected things she heard here and there, barely audible phrases caught by accident, through closed doors, from the kitchen, in mangled phone conversations; plus there's what she was told directly, which she knows is only partial, and as such, a lie. *Corruption of minors*, she heard, although later she learned that expression wasn't used anymore. These days the phrase is *crimes against sexual freedom*. It sounds strange, because Soon didn't even know that she had sexuality, much less any freedom regarding it. For her it was all—is all—incomprehensible. She blushes at the mere thought that they asked him the same questions as her. Was there touching? Did he take pictures of you? Did he ask you to take your clothes off—some or all of them? Did he take his clothes off? Did he show you videos or photos of other children? Or of other adults committing obscene acts? The policeman who asked the questions treated her gently, but he didn't beat around the bush. Her mother, sitting beside her, translated for her in a low voice. *Obscene* means *dirty*, things you shouldn't do with your body, things that make you ashamed or feel bad. No, no, no, Soon said, disturbed. But, what about the things she wrote in her notebook . . . ? She went silent. Why had she written such things? Should she admit she made them up? Was that the same thing as admitting she'd committed an *obscene* act? Soon was silent, holding back her tears, and that only emphasized—no doubt about it—that she was hiding something.

Don't be scared, her father told her later, and then she heard him whisper to her mother: she's protecting him, *that dirty old man*. That pervert. That degenerate.

(But Old Man hadn't done anything. She hadn't either, really. She'd only written it. Her round, childish handwriting had turned dangerous, accusatory.)

Old Man toys with the paper napkins. He tears them into strips, rolls them around his chubby fingers and makes rings out of them, one on each finger. They'd asked him the same questions as her, surely, but in a different, cruder tone, without meeting his eyes, and he'd had no mother there to translate. He refused to give a statement, she'd heard them say. A guilty silence, his, because not to talk is to confess. He who is silent concedes.

Old Man isn't going to give her the details. He's not going to tell her anything about those days. He would love to go back to talking about birds. That's the only thing he says. He misses it! Does Soon know that just a few days ago they found a new species of finch? There were only three hundred of them left in the world, so few that they were unclassified! Incredible, because their color is extraordinary, pure blue, a clean, sharp blue. They could have gone extinct and no one, never ever, would have recorded their existence in the world!

Soon asks him to tell her more about the bird. Where it lives. How big it is. What it eats. Old Man answers everything with a touch of pride, like a child who has learned his lesson well. Soon is still fascinated by his ability to memorize information, but now she sees him from another side, as if she were older than him.

She'd also been told that Old Man was retarded, but she wants to believe that's a lie, like everything else. Or almost everything.

Precisely because of the matter of Old Man, no one was too worried about her missing school. They insinuated that it could have been Old Man who encouraged her to skip, possibly with coercion and threats. She insists it was her own decision, but even so it took them a long time to believe her, or they never did believe her, and in any case the whole thing—her truancy—ended up swept under the rug, as if it hadn't been the root of everything, even the seed. Now Soon does go to school, she doesn't miss a single day—her teachers must have been told to report any absence immediately. Now that Marga isn't there and Soon is no longer a marshmallow, school is bearable. She's still annoyed by group work, but it's just a matter of getting used to it, her teacher says. Everything will go back to normal, she adds, though Soon doesn't understand what she means by *normal*. Practically all the girls in her class have boyfriends—the ones who had them last year have now replaced them with new ones—and a lot have slept with them. She's realized by now that *sleep with* doesn't just mean *lay down beside*, but rather doing many other things that approach her mother's description of *obscene acts*. Still, those girls are not monitored by their teachers, and if they miss school they're not reported immediately, as she would be. Alongside these other girls Soon is still a little strange, and it's possible that she'll have to find a boyfriend soon so she won't stand out so much. The day she starts going with someone her age she will start to forget about Old Man, about what they call her Stockholm syndrome, how in reality she was in love with him, and how she forgives him and even makes excuses for him, how she's been traumatized ever since it happened, how her attitude is unhealthy and abnormal. The toll she will have to pay, though, will be high. She's not sure she wants to go with anyone, much less sleep with them. In her diary she'd nonchalantly written that she'd slept with Old Man, but she meant lay down beside him and let him touch her. Writing that was horrible, it seems, but doing it with anyone her own age, that's apparently fine, and is apparently what's expected of her.

Retarded is not the word they used when they talked to her, but Soon heard it several times, especially at first, when her parents were so worried and so, so angry that they didn't even bite their tongues in her presence: *moron, idiot, crazy,* interchangeably. *Mentally challenged,* they called him later, and also a person with *mental retardation,* which is less insulting than *retarded*. Of all their accusations, Soon thinks this one is the most absurd. Old Man has an intelligence that other people don't understand, that's all. How many of them are capable of retaining the names of thousands of birds in Latin, and of listing their characteristics one by one? Could they recognize and distinguish those birds' songs—do they have an ear for those subtleties? And Nina Simone's songs, word for word, all the lyrics without even knowing English? And her life in detail, her biography broken down month by month? Old Man runs circles around them all.

Not long ago, in art history class, they learned about Van Gogh. The teacher said that today he is considered a genius, but when he was alive people thought he was crazy and even retarded. Sometimes he got agitated and made trouble in the neighborhood. He cut off a piece of his own ear. He ended up killing himself. Old Man hasn't cut anything off, at least not that she knows of, and he hasn't hurt anyone. Still, people call him retarded too, though for other reasons. Her mother sat her down, tried to explain politely so as not to shock her. That man, she said, was born with a birth defect, a defect that can't be cured. It happens in certain families, when children are born in a way they shouldn't be. In small families, she added, that mix among themselves. It's possible that it's given him a confused idea of things. Of relationships. It's not entirely his fault, but that doesn't mean it's okay for him to associate with a girl like her. People like him, she went on, should be subject to more control. They're victims, but they can also be wrongdoers. Then she heard her father grumbling in the other room. Victims, victims, he repeated, weighting the word with irony and contempt. Her father never sat down with her to explain anything about Old Man. It put him on edge, he said, drove him crazy just to think about what might have happened. My little girl, my little girl, he said.

Oddly, during those days, her father stopped calling her by her name. She started to be his *child* and then, even more frequently, *my little girl*. He was much more affected than her mother by everything that happened. That's what Soon overheard in several conversations. She's *his little girl*, Soon's mother would say, his only girl, and he's devastated. That a man—an old man—would put his hands on *your little girl*— the very idea that an old man could put his hands on your little girl—it's enough to drive any man crazy, everyone can understand that. He doesn't care a whit if the man in question wasn't in his right mind. Plus, the man had proven to be perfectly aware of his actions. But, what actions? Only the ones they'd managed to prove. And which ones were those, to be exact? Then the conversation went downhill.

Later, her father started to look at her suspiciously, afraid that she also held, inside her, the seed of rot. She saw him doubt, embrace, and then furiously let go of the idea of her innocence. He came into her room and tore up her beautiful bird poster. Since when have you liked birds?, he asked. Rats with wings, nasty creatures, disgusting, he said as he shredded the poster. He also searched her shelves and closet, dispensed with anything he suspected might have come from

Old Man. And his distrust seemed endless, it lasted several weeks. Until he calmed down. More or less, he calmed down. To maintain that calm, it's true, everyone avoided the use of certain uncomfortable words, words that had always been harmless before: *diary*, especially, but also *notebook*, *park*, *bird*, and even *sausage*. No one wrote a list of forbidden terms; there was no need: the three of them—father, mother, and Soon—knew full well what they were.

They told her so many things. Like about how he'd been in the mental hospital for assaulting the woman at the bird sanctuary. Like about his mental retardation and his birth defect. Also that he went through periods of alcoholism and that he'd been arrested several times for various violent episodes. He'd damaged public property and intimidated passersby, some of them minors. *Violent episode* is just as confusing a phrase as *obscene act* or *public property*, though in this case no one explained it to her, and Soon remained in the dark. Self-harm: several instances. Suicide attempts: two. The first one she already knew about, at the mental hospital: he managed to steal rat poison and swallowed all he could. Now she thinks of that friend of his who'd hung himself and left his clothes to Old Man, and wonders: was it common to kill yourself in the mental hospital? Maybe Old Man had tried that method—hanging—in his second attempt, the details of which are not recorded. Soon has secretly read the report the lawyer gave her parents. It detailed these precedents in order to provide a basis for the case, but it was written in such a rigid and euphemistic way that Soon could barely interpret it. At first her parents were all in, which is why they hired such a meticulous lawyer. They wanted to bring Old Man to trial and put him behind bars for as long as possible. A man like that is a danger to the public, they said. They must have thought better of it later. Because of the diary and what it implied, because if it couldn't be used as proof . . . what could it be used for, then?

The diary complicates things, dirties them. It's better to ignore it, forget about it. No one talks about the diary now. It doesn't even occur to her to write another one—what for? Recording the life she leads would be very boring, and imagination—at least for now—is forbidden her.

Still, as she looks at Old Man—as she observes his protruding cheekbones and his yellow skin, his elegant but dirty two-piece suit—the diary is present again, there between them. Why did she write all of that? The prickle of guilt is insistent. She has no choice but to face it, and confess.

They read my diary, she finally explains. Old Man looks at her, without comprehending at first. Then he says: oh, that. In the diary, Soon talked about Old Man, she talked about the hideout in the park, about the park workers, the rainy days and the cold days, and how those days were becoming a problem. She talked about the snacks they ate, with very slight variations, of course—*champagne, cocaine, and sausages*—and about some other minor matters—presents, towels, fabrications: this part she's not going to tell him, it's too brutal.

It's possible that they read the diary because they already suspected something was off, at least since the appearance of that policeman who'd presented them with the summons from the education inspectorate—or was it from social services? They suspected, yes, her mother must have called her teacher in the end and found out about Soon missing school. But what they couldn't even imagine was what that diary held, which was truth and lies, but basically a form of truth. Their surprise must have been great, even greater than their fear, because they'd taken their time before acting and they'd gotten advice, Soon has no doubt about that. If they asked her about it too soon, her parents were told, they ran the risk of scaring her, and the crime—because they were already thinking in terms of a crime—would go unpunished. The diary didn't contain enough information to identify the criminal, and what it did say was confusing and even contradictory. It was better to catch them red-handed. Or almost red-handed: about to get blood on their hands.

Now Soon is frightened to think how that last morning, while she was packing her backpack in order to go on deceiving her parents, it was them, her parents, who were deceiving her by pretending everything was normal. She didn't sense anything, noticed nothing out of the ordinary when she left her house and started down the same street as always, until she reached the moment when her route to school was adulterated and became the route to the park—a moment when her parents, who were following at a distance, must have felt their hearts start pounding. She saw the same people she did every day, complacent now in her routine, with earphones isolating her from the world—*southern trees bearing strange fruit, blood on the leaves and blood at the roots*—looking down at her sneakers to avoid meeting anyone's eyes. Then she reached the park.

Now she stops talking. She's realized that, as she recalls that day, she's making Old Man remember his own part. She sees his hands are trembling—his hands with their rings of twisted paper. He has placed one over the other to curb the shaking, or to hide it. And what else, Soon?, he asks. Did they capture you, did they hurt you?

It's uncomfortable to admit that they treated her with all the delicacy they most likely denied him. No, they didn't do anything to her, she says, they didn't even scold her. If it weren't for Old Man, if it were just about skipping school for almost three months, she would have gotten it good. But thanks to Old Man she received only sweetness and understanding—even if it was a twisted sweetness and understanding, employed solely to coax a confession out of her. She got really scared when she heard the hedges move and it wasn't Old Man who appeared, but her mother and then her father, both their faces fallen. Oh my god, oh my god, her mother repeated, clutching her head, though there was nothing about the scene to warrant such a reaction: just her daughter, just Soon, sitting calmly at the foot of a tree, taking out her earphones, utterly bewildered.

They whisked her away from there without a single question. Her father talked on the phone in a low voice while her mother told her it was all over, she was finally safe. Yes, said her father to whomever was on the other end of the line: she's fine, just a little scared, my wife is taking her home now.

Old Man trembles as he takes over the story. Now I know, I get it now! When he entered the park, he noticed there was something strange in the atmosphere. Something heavy and dark, as if the air were full of ashes. The birds were quiet, either they'd flown far away or they could sense what was coming! As he approached the hideout, he could see the dark color of police uniforms—bad memories!—but even then he didn't understand. He never had time to react. A crowd of them advanced on him, as if he were armed! They surrounded him!

What was Soon doing while they were putting him in handcuffs and taking him away in the van? She was pretending. She couldn't gather the strength to protest. Her mother hugged her, cried disconsolately, and apologized for not having been able to take care of her as she deserved.

Soon didn't understand anything.

For some time now the waitress hasn't taken her eyes off them. Three hours? Three and a half? How long have those two, Soon and Old Man, been sitting there without consuming anything? When they sat down they ordered two sodas, which they drank with their eyes downcast, not exchanging a single word. Then they started to talk, and since then they haven't stopped. But their way of conversing is strange to any outside observer. First one of them talks and the other listens, for a while. Then the other way around. It's not exactly a dialogue, more like an exchange of monologues, each one with their subject, unrelated and unreplied-to. Now the old man has started to tremble, and his eyes are closed: the girl has hurt him. The waitress watches them and it occurs to Soon, suddenly, that she could call the authorities, and that the second offense would be viewed in a different light—a worse light. She has to deflect the waitress's attention, get things back on track and in order. Old Man, Old Man, she whispers, let's forget about all this, it's not worth going on. Why don't you tell me something about Nina Simone. Something you've never told me before.

It takes Old Man a while to answer, but the shaking of his hands subsides, his eyes twinkle again, and after a couple of minutes, he finally manages to speak. There was a Colombian choreographer, he says, who staged a dance performance in honor of Nina. It was called "Negra slash Anger." Not slash spelled out, but the backslash symbol! And it was a performance about racism. Nina Simone's daughter, Lisa Simone, was going to see the show in Cartagena de Indias—where there's still so much racism! Yes, he has read up on the population there, how many are black, how many mixed, how many Palenqueros, how many indigenous, or with unclear ethnicity. He gives her numbers, percentages, which Soon doesn't listen to. In the end, Old Man goes on, Lisa couldn't go because there was a hurricane and her flight was cancelled. Bad luck! But Lisa is a good daughter. She has taken up her mother's legacy. She sings and denounces inequality. She's a good daughter!

They didn't choose that particular cafe because they liked it, but just because it was the closest one, only a few feet away from where they happened to run into each other. It was Soon who recognized him first—he was wearing the same suit, the same shoes, though he's so thin! He blinked a few seconds before he fully realized who this girl who'd called out to him was, this girl who was looking him up and down, smiling, fearful, glancing around just in case, come on, Old Man, come on, we could go in here for a while.

A cafe to have a snack, frequented by girls like the one Soon will be in a few years—or months!—and parents with their children and coffees and fruit smoothies. Could Old Man play that role, the role of Soon's father? No, he couldn't. The relationship between them is conspicuously different. Lateral and suspicious. An old man who has nothing to hide doesn't start to tremble sitting across from a teenager. And a teenager who no longer looks like a marshmallow doesn't waste her time with a guy who goes around dressed like that, like Old Man. The waitress must be having thoughts along those lines. Luckily, she also has a lot of work, she's the only waitress for all the tables; luckily as well Old Man's expression has changed by now, he no longer looks forlorn but excited, and it's all because of Nina Simone, or because Soon keeps asking him—avidly—about Nina Simone.

(If the waitress had to point out the guilty one in that relationship, she wouldn't hesitate for a second: Old Man, with his outdated suit and the paper napkins rolled around his fingers.)

Her brother had returned from abroad. He rushed back as soon as he found out—as soon as they told him—about the mess his little sister had gotten into, about the man who had corrupted her, the retarded—mentally handicapped—old man who'd been locked up before for assaulting another woman, and who had encouraged her to skip school—or had forced her to skip under who knows what kind of coercion—the man who'd confused her and driven her crazy and isolated her from her friends, the one who's made Soon, his little sister, so disoriented and strange. Her brother caught the first plane back and came straight home, worried, very worried. He hugged her fearfully. But Soon wonders about the sense of that return, now that it was less necessary than ever. He was different, Old Man, she tells him. It was like he wasn't her brother, but an older man, much older than her, one who knew perfectly well what was good for her and what wasn't. He didn't come to give me support, says Soon: he came to give me advice. She heard him talking to her parents at night, after she was already in bed, the three of them conspiring against her, analyzing her feelings, her reactions, reversing how it was in the past—because it used to be them, Soon and her brother, who conspired against their parents, never the other way around. Not only had she lost her ally, but that ally had now turned against her, enlisted in the opposing forces. He spent three or four days at home, but Soon doesn't know what for. He came and went, talking constantly on the phone. Soon suspected that he told the story—his version of the story—to everyone he could, to see if they could give his little sister a hand. Her adult brother had been corrupted and didn't know how to keep a secret anymore. In other times Soon would have broken, she would have confessed about the diary and how unfair everything had been for Old Man because of her. But that was a different time. Now she had no choice but to keep quiet and comply. It's okay, big bro, you can go back to your life feeling fine, it's all under control, you've helped me a lot by coming. That man, visibly satisfied by a job well done, caught his plane home and left as hurriedly as he'd come. But this time, Soon bore his departure with indifference. I don't blame him, she tells Old Man: he's not the same, but neither am I.

For months, they took Soon to see a psychologist. She was a very friendly woman who spoke softly and gave the impression she doubted everything, even herself. She stammered, she hemmed and hawed, and she contradicted herself all the time. She talked about certain things with Soon and other, totally different things with Soon's parents—Soon came to this conclusion after eavesdropping one day. The psychologist told her parents that she, Soon, was very confused. That the problem had started a long time ago, though it was impossible to determine its cause. That she felt panic at the onset of her sexuality and that, unconsciously, she had sought an ally in an older man who, when the moment came, she could manipulate as she liked. This last part was what had most outraged her father. *Soon* manipulated the *old man*? More like the other way around!, she heard him murmur through the door. Her mother soothed him, told him it was a matter of terminology: the point was that it was *unconscious*, of course the child couldn't control anyone. Hidden, Soon listened and bit her tongue to keep from interrupting. She had never talked to the psychologist about any of that! She just answered her questions about hobbies, tastes, and desires for the future, the kind of questions adults ask kids they don't know how to talk to: what's your favorite subject, what do you want to be when you grow up, what's your greatest life dream? The psychologist couldn't know how rebellious Soon was in her answers. She talked about birds and Nina Simone, tried to disconcert and surprise her: her favorite subject was natural sciences, she wanted to be an ornithologist when she grew up, her greatest dream was to go back in time and hear Nina sing live. But she had never talked about sexuality—why did the psychologist take everything she said straight to that stuff? After the day she listened to her parents through the door, she started to look at the psychologist differently. Her innocent air, her skin, so white, and her melancholic green eyes now held a perversion that repelled her. That woman was sick, Soon thought: sick with psychology. She refused to talk to her anymore, and in the end her parents cancelled the sessions.

Although in one session they did talk about the diary. The psychiatrist asked her how long she'd been writing it. She didn't remember, Soon said. She only wrote in it off and on. There were periods when she wrote a lot and others when she didn't write at all, absolutely nothing. And what caused those intervals? Did she write when she felt bad or when she felt good? The latter: when she felt good. So, what she wrote about that man . . . ? Soon said nothing. She didn't understand the question. What was the question? The psychologist blinked. When you wrote about that man, did you feel good? Soon said no, then yes, then that it wasn't easy to explain: she was cornered. Because, the psychologist went on, you wrote repugnant things. I copied them, said Soon. Copied them from where? Did you copy them or were they dictated to you? Did that man dictate them? Did he ask you to write them so he could read them later? The psychologist was sounding like a cop: her inquisitive tone, formulistic and accusatory. Soon shrank in her chair, pressed against the backrest; she wanted to run away. I copied them from a book, she stammered. A book I found in the library. The psychologist looked at her seriously for a few seconds, in silence. Then a faint grimace emerged, which ended up becoming a smile, a sweet smile. You mustn't worry, she said: it's not bad to imagine things, the only problem is that sometimes our imagination runs away and certain bad people can take advantage of our lack of control. Soon nodded without understanding. The psychologist repeated that she shouldn't worry in the slightest about the matter of the diary. But Soon thought: if that's true, why did she bring it up. She couldn't forget the serious way the woman had looked at her before absolving her. That sternness had contained an extremely severe judgement, one part reprobation and another part disgust. To the psychologist, Soon must be like a girl possessed by the devil.

She doesn't tell Old Man about any of this, either. No, they didn't medicate her by force, or stick her in isolation, or tie her to a chair. But she felt humiliated in a different way. The only thing she says to him is: who are they to think they can understand us? Old Man says: to them we're like stuffed chickens! They cut us open and empty us out and then fill us up with whatever they think is better, and into the oven we go! Cooked to psychology's order!

Right then the waitress interrupts them, placing her hand on the table between them, her arm with the sleeve rolled up, the striped shirt, a bunch of brightly colored bracelets, their invasive tinkling. *Cooked to psychology's order!*, is what he is saying right then, and the waitress: kids—kids!—you can't take up a table this long without buying anything, I'm afraid if you don't order something else you'll have to leave. Sure, sure, concedes Old Man. Sorry, murmurs Soon. Neither of them looks up—they stare instead at the arm, that fateful executioner's arm. I'll give you five minutes, she announces as she turns around, her voice dry, cutting, categorical. The countdown begins.

Remember when we talked about getting married?, says Old Man, half-closing his eyes, rushing through the final moments. Yeah, says Soon, and she feels profoundly embarrassed. He reaches his hands toward her, his fingers crowned with paper rings. In the bird sanctuary where he worked, he tells her, he used to help the keeper ring birds. It was like a kind of wedding, a union until death! Ringing birds is a job that demands extreme care, their feet are all so delicate and fragile! He'd found the rings beautiful. Light, made of aluminum, with the pertinent numbers imprinted so no one could forget where, when, or by whom each specimen was ringed. A bird that is ringed here could appear years later and ten thousand kilometers away. It can happen! Thanks to that tiny little ring, we can track a lot of information: where the bird migrated, how long it lived, what it ate, and how it died. One time, he caught a shearwater that had been ringed fifty years before. You see, Soon? Fifty years! It would be good if the two of them could wear rings like that their whole lives. Even if they never saw each other again, it would be known when and why they put them on. But there are no rings like that for people. No one rings someone before letting them fly free, like they used to—the keeper and Old Man—at the sanctuary, with the birds.

Old Man takes off the rolled-up paper rings, one by one, and as he does he tears them up, leaving the table covered in shredded paper. Finally there's only one left, the one on his ring finger, which he wiggles up and down, pointing it at her. Want it?, he finally says. She laughs, nods. But then she'll have to make another one for him, they should exchange them, like in real weddings! Still laughing, Soon takes a napkin, tears it into strips, rolls one of the strips between two fingers into the shape of a ring. Here, she says, and as she says it she glances at the waitress, who by now is furious, because their five minutes are up and there the two of them still sit, degrading the place, playing with bits of paper, getting everything messy, interlacing their fingers with no respect, no decorum, disobeying authority. She sees them get up: the ridiculous, pathetic old man who looks spaced out and sick, and the scruffy girl, with her oversized clothes that she thinks hide her extra kilos, a neurotic girl, weird and naive. She watches them walk to the door, now without a glance her way, without even waving goodbye, without thanking her for the grace period she granted them, going out to the street absorbed in themselves, an unacceptable, illogical pair, stopping a little further down on the narrow, dirty sidewalk, looking at each other without speaking, without touching, and then they turn, each one heading in their own direction, the old man to the right, downcast, asymmetrical, with his crazy-person walk, toward the past; the girl to the left, downcast, asymmetrical, with her crazy-person walk, toward the future.

Author's Note

The novella *Among the Hedges* has its seed in the story "A contrapelo," which I wrote for the anthology *Riesgo,* published by :Rata_ press in 2017. In its shift to this new text, the characters have gone through significant modifications and the narrative is different, but if anyone were to want to trace its origin, it is there, in that story.

The conversation between Soon and Old Man about the existence of a bird without feet is practically identical to a scene in the play *Orpheus Descending,* by Tennessee Williams, though I must admit that my first knowledge of this beautiful metaphor came from the play's film adaptation, *The Fugitive Kind,* directed by Sidney Lumet and starring Anna Magnani and Marlon Brando.

Although the story, characters, and settings of *Among the Hedges* are completely invented, as I was writing I was picturing certain areas of Amate Park and its surroundings in Seville, where I often used to walk back when I was Soon's age, a long time ago.

SARA MESA is the author of eleven works, including the novels *Scar* (winner of the Ojo Critico Prize), *Four by Four* (a finalist for the Herralde Prize), *An Invisible Fire* (winner of the Premio Málaga de Novela), *Un Amor*, and *Among the Hedges*. Her works have been translated into more than ten different languages, and she has been widely praised for her concise, sharp writing style.

MEGAN MCDOWELL has translated many of the most important Latin American writers working today, including Samanta Schweblin and Alejandro Zambra. Her translations have won the English PEN award and the Premio Valle-Inclán, and been nominated three times for the International Booker Prize. Her short story translations have been featured in *The New Yorker*, *The Paris Review*, *Tin House*, *McSweeney's*, and *Granta*, among others. In 2020 she won an Award in Literature from the American Academy of Arts and Letters. She lives in Santiago, Chile.

Inga Ābele (Latvia)
  High Tide
Naja Marie Aidt (Denmark)
  Rock, Paper, Scissors
Esther Allen et al. (ed.) (World)
  *The Man Between: Michael Henry
  Heim & a Life in Translation*
Bae Suah (South Korea)
  A Greater Music
  North Station
Zsófia Bán (Hungarian)
  Night School
Svetislav Basara (Serbia)
  The Cyclist Conspiracy
Michal Ben-Naftali (Israel)
  The Teacher
Guðbergur Bergsson (Iceland)
  Tómas Jónsson, Bestseller
Max Besora (Catalonia)
  *The Adventures and Misadventures
  of Joan Orpí . . .*
Jean-Marie Blas de Roblès (World)
  Island of Point Nemo
Per Aage Brandt (Denmark)
  If I Were a Suicide Bomber
Can Xue (China)
  Frontier
  Vertical Motion
Lúcio Cardoso (Brazil)
  Chronicle of the Murdered House
Sergio Chejfec (Argentina)
  The Dark
  The Incompletes
  My Two Worlds
  The Planets
Eduardo Chirinos (Peru)
  The Smoke of Distant Fires
Manuela Draeger (France)
  Eleven Sooty Dreams
Marguerite Duras (France)
  Abahn Sabana David
  L'Amour
  The Sailor from Gibraltar
Elisa Shua Dusapin (France)
  Winter in Sokcho
Mathias Énard (France)
  Street of Thieves
  Zone
Macedonio Fernández (Argentina)
  The Museum of Eterna's Novel
Rubem Fonseca (Brazil)
  The Taker & Other Stories
Rodrigo Fresán (Argentina)
  The Bottom of the Sky
  The Dreamed Part
  The Invented Part

Juan Gelman (Argentina)
  Dark Times Filled with Light
Oliverio Girondo (Argentina)
  Decals
Georgi Gospodinov (Bulgaria)
  The Physics of Sorrow
Arnon Grunberg (Netherlands)
  Tirza
Hubert Haddad (France)
  *Rochester Knockings:
  A Novel of the Fox Sisters*
Gail Hareven (Israel)
  Lies, First Person
Angel Igov (Bulgaria)
  A Short Tale of Shame
Ilya Ilf & Evgeny Petrov (Russia)
  The Golden Calf
Zachary Karabashliev (Bulgaria)
  18% Gray
Ha Seong-nan (South Korea)
  Bluebeard's First Wife
  Flowers of Mold
Hristo Karastoyanov (Bulgaria)
  The Same Night Awaits Us All
Jan Kjærstad (Norway)
  The Conqueror
  The Discoverer
Josefine Klougart (Denmark)
  One of Us Is Sleeping
Carlos Labbé (Chile)
  Loquela
  Navidad & Matanza
  Spiritual Choreographies
Lee Soho (Korea)
  Catcalling
Jakov Lind (Austria)
  Ergo
  Landscape in Concrete
Andri Snær Magnason (Iceland)
  On Time and Water
Andreas Maier (Germany)
  Klausen
Lucio Mariani (Italy)
  Traces of Time
Sara Mesa (Spain)
  Among the Hedges
  Four by Four
Amanda Michalopoulou (Greece)
  Why I Killed My Best Friend
Valerie Miles (World)
  A Thousand Forests in One Acorn
Subimal Misra (India)
  *This Could Have Become Ramayan
  Chamar's Tale*
Iben Mondrup (Denmark)
  Justine

Quim Monzó (Catalonia)
  Gasoline
  Guadalajara
  A Thousand Morons
  Why, Why, Why?
Elsa Morante (Italy)
  Aracoeli
Giulio Mozzi (Italy)
  This Is the Garden
Andrés Neuman (Spain)
  The Things We Don't Do
Jóanes Nielsen (Faroe Islands)
  The Brahmadells
Madame Nielsen (Denmark)
  The Endless Summer
Henrik Nordbrandt (Denmark)
  When We Leave Each Other
Asta Olivia Nordenhof (Denmark)
  The Easiness and the Loneliness
Wojciech Nowicki (Poland)
  Salki
Bragi Ólafsson (Iceland)
  The Ambassador
  Narrator
  The Pets
Kristín Ómarsdóttir (Iceland)
  Children in Reindeer Woods
Sigrún Pálsdóttir (Iceland)
  History. A Mess.
Diego Trelles Paz (ed.) (World)
  The Future Is Not Ours
Ilja Leonard Pfeijffer (Netherlands)
  Rupert: A Confession
Jerzy Pilch (Poland)
  The Mighty Angel
  My First Suicide
  A Thousand Peaceful Cities
Rein Raud (Estonia)
  The Brother
João Reis (Portugal)
  The Translator's Bride
Rainer Maria Rilke (World)
  Sonnets to Orpheus
Mónica Ramón Ríos (Chile)
  Cars on Fire
Mercè Rodoreda (Catalonia)
  Camellia Street
  Death in Spring
  Garden by the Sea
  The Selected Stories of Mercè Rodoreda
  War, So Much War
Milen Ruskov (Bulgaria)
  Thrown into Nature
Guillermo Saccomanno (Argentina)
  77
  The Clerk
  Gesell Dome

Juan José Saer (Argentina)
  The Clouds
  La Grande
  The One Before
  The Regal Lemon Tree
  Scars
  The Sixty-Five Years of Washington
Olga Sedakova (Russia)
  In Praise of Poetry
Mikhail Shishkin (Russia)
  Maidenhair
Sölvi Björn Sigurðsson (Iceland)
  The Last Days of My Mother
Maria José Silveira (Brazil)
  *Her Mother's Mother's Mother and
    Her Daughters*
Andrzej Sosnowski (Poland)
  Lodgings
Albena Stambolova (Bulgaria)
  Everything Happens as It Does
Benjamin Stein (Germany)
  The Canvas
Georgi Tenev (Bulgaria)
  Party Headquarters
Dubravka Ugresic (Europe)
  The Age of Skin
  American Fictionary
  Europe in Sepia
  Fox
  Karaoke Culture
  Nobody's Home
Ludvík Vaculík (Czech Republic)
  The Guinea Pigs
Jorge Volpi (Mexico)
  Season of Ash
Antoine Volodine (France)
  Bardo or Not Bardo
  *Post-Exoticism in Ten Lessons,
    Lesson Eleven*
  Radiant Terminus
Eliot Weinberger (ed.) (World)
  Elsewhere
Ingrid Winterbach (South Africa)
  The Book of Happenstance
  The Elusive Moth
  To Hell with Cronjé
Ror Wolf (Germany)
  Two or Three Years Later
Words Without Borders (ed.) (World)
  The Wall in My Head
Xiao Hong (China)
  Ma Bo'le's Second Life
Alejandro Zambra (Chile)
  The Private Lives of Trees